The Fifth Man

Bani Basu

Translated from the Bengali by Arunava Sinha

PENGUIN BOOKS
An imprint of Penguin Random House

PENGUIN BOOKS

USA | Canada | UK | Ireland | Australia
New Zealand | India | South Africa | China | Singapore

Penguin Books is part of the Penguin Random House group of companies whose addresses can be found at global.penguinrandomhouse.com

Published by Penguin Random House India Pvt. Ltd
4th Floor, Capital Tower 1, MG Road,
Gurugram 122 002, Haryana, India

Penguin Random House India

First published by Random House India 2014
Published in Penguin Books by Penguin Random House India 2018

10 9 8 7 6 5 4 3 2

ISBN 9788184005721

Typeset in Sabon by R. Ajith Kumar

Printed at Manipal Technologies Limited, India

www.penguin.co.in

FSC www.fsc.org
MIX
Paper | Supporting responsible forestry
FSC® C043100

This is a legitimate digitally printed version of the book and therefore might not have certain extra finishing on the cover.

To
Durgadas Chattopadhyay

ONE

Aritra had woken up after a strange dream, recovering slowly in a room suffused by blue light. The curtains at the head of his bed were drawn. Like a torrent of water impeded by boulders, the street light had rushed in through the opening, and the blue night-lamp had faded. The blue of the earthly sky. In the dead of night, his sparsely-furnished room had silently merged in its entirety with the external world. The room was no longer recognizable as a room, its six walls seemed to have fallen away. There was only a white strip on the window near the head. The entire western wall was an eagle with unfurled wings. More wide open windows. A desolate emptiness and the sense of an enormous expanse. Not the room but the world, not the world but the sky when it is blue. The sky itself. Uniting sleep and wakefulness, dream and reality. Was it a night of strong winds? And so, formless dreams had arrived at the junction between sleep and oblivion. The night wind had separated the physical Aritra from the mental one, overcoming space-time. Somewhere between deep and light slumber, something moved in a flash from ignorance to knowledge, like a bolt of lightning, before it disappeared. Some dreams are clear remnants of certain wishes, fears, rages and desires. Tamarind seeds used for indoor games were scattered across the terrain of consciousness. But this wasn't that sort of dream. Someone had appeared, to say something. Sleep had no ears. So it had to be said through visual symbols.

Now light sleep and wakefulness were celebrating their union. Listening to the cries of triumph, Aritra felt he was much taller than his six foot frame. His feet had stretched to where the sun sets in the west, his arms were exploring the eastern horizon, getting longer and longer. His memory and identity had expanded many, many miles beyond the limits of the past and the future. His mental self floated in an ocean of space with no compass points. So wakefulness was the real state of sleep. Only one tiny cell remained animate. And sleep was an awakened state of the consciousness. Where one could find oneself, but only after losing oneself in a huge explosion.

Aritra couldn't locate his limbs when he woke up. Only the sense of 'I am Aritra' dangled loosely somewhere near his mind. At any other time he would have been afraid. Especially since he had been close to literally losing his legs in a terrifying scooter accident. But Aritra was not frightened. He was perfectly aware that he was neither lying on a road in Shivajinagar with twisted limbs, nor unable to regain consciousness after his surgery at Sassoon Hospital. Only if he could maintain this fearless state would he be able to recognize in its entirety the momentary dream that had flashed in the deepest recess of his sleep, taking the form of a ghostly cuneiform script before vanishing. Only then would he able to retrieve it. *Nannyah pantha vidyate*. There is no other path to eternal life. Therefore Aritra closed his eyes again. In case he could go back to sleep, that sleep which was really awakening. Once more. Somewhere far away a bird of dawn was calling irresistibly. Aritra tried to return, riding this sweet romanticism. But the blue sky quickly changed its colours, donning the pallid robe of dawn. The resident gods of the arms and legs and chest and back and stomach and voice returned to their kingdoms. A tall mirror against the wall at one end of the room shimmered as though it were floating to the surface of the water. Next to it a mid-sized table, on it medicine bottles of different sizes, and on the opposite wall, arranged in a half-moon configuration, the Last Supper, the Burial of Christ, and the Pietà—three paintings of Christ, no one knew the reason behind this sublimity of sin, death and betrayal in the bedroom—and, seated in profile on the chair in front of the table with her forehead resting on her hand, a sleepless Neelam in a turquoise nightdress. Her close-cropped curly hair usually resembled a halo of mist in the morning. This was Neelam's distinguishing feature. Aritra called it Neelam's Aureole. Her head usually acquired this shape soon after she had attended to her hair. The reason was simple. Neelam had some juvenile hair which had vowed since birth never to grow. Although, some of them had had no qualms about greying in infancy. The second reason was Neelam's habit of shaking her head violently.

The chirping of morning birds from the cluster of trees in the field behind the house was getting louder. Opening his eyes a quarter of the way and watching Neelam intently, Aritra tried to understand how long, just how long she had been sitting there. He had not seen her come in; her eyes were sunken. Had she sat there all night, then? Why? Aritra was much better now. There was no question of watching over him constantly. He went to the bathroom without help, though he still had to drag his left leg a little. Two sections had been amputated from the index and ring fingers of his right hand. In other words, the god figure had deprived him of the right to threaten anyone for the rest of his life. If he wanted to wear a ring it would have to be on the left hand. But Aritra had recovered completely. In fact, long rest and attention had practically given him a new life. There was no need for anxiety. Why then was Neelam sitting that way? She seemed to have collapsed, with her head in her hands. Engrossed in thought. Aritra wanted to ask, 'Did you have the same dream that I did, Neelam?' Was it possible to have the same dream at the same time except in a fairy-tale? Neelam would be needlessly flustered if asked. Aritra had been quite delusional after the accident. So he just shifted in his bed without a word. He had been lying on his left side, facing Neelam and the table. Now he turned towards the Last Supper and the Pietà. At once Neelam rose to her feet, like someone still in a dream. Coming up to him, she said, 'Are you up? Will you get up? Shall I bring you some tea?'

These were the words she uttered, but Aritra seemed to hear Neelam say, 'Are you listening? Will you listen?

Listen to me quickly.' Anxiety was writ large on her face. Aritra answered the unasked questions, saying, 'Yes, tell me.' Neelam started. Then she said, 'Did you hear anything last night?'

'Hear what?'

'Mahanam-ji passed through this road. Mahanam-ji is here.'

Sitting up in bed, Aritra shook off the sheet he had been sleeping under. 'What are you saying, Neelam?' he said. 'Tell me clearly.'

Neelam's voice was trembling. 'You didn't hear a car horn outside our gate around 2 a.m., did you? Shambha-ji, the new night guard, rang our bell, saying, some people are here, looking for you. I said, I'll come and check, don't unlock the gate. He had got out of the car, he was standing outside. Even from a distance I knew who it was, but I couldn't make out his form properly in the darkness. When I reached the gate Mahanam-ji said, the road booming with his voice, well, Neelam? Were you scared to send Ari? I didn't tell him anything about your accident, all I said was, I'll tell them to open the gate, come in. So late, though? What's the matter? Did you miss the Sahyadri Express? Mahanam-ji said, there are so many things I've missed. My destiny is missing my chances. So there's nothing to fear. Go back to sleep happily. I'm going towards Pimpri. That's where I'm staying.'

'Staying with whom?' Aritra asked. 'At Pimpri! If it's a Bengali we should know them.'

'I don't know,' answered Neelam. 'Whom do we know who has a white Fiat there? I couldn't make out anything more in the darkness. He entered and exited so dramatically.'

Aritra frowned, telling himself, 'That's his tactic. But it won't checkmate me anymore.' To Neelam he said, 'Will you get me some tea?'

As soon as Neelam left the room there was a clap of thunder in Aritra's head. Against a light blue backdrop, something like a dark blue room, a cave. Two black birds flying out of it with outspread wings. Maintaining a fixed distance and an identical rhythm, as though attached to each other by a thread. After a while they begin to retreat, slowly. And then disappear in a flash. That was the dream. Now on his dishevelled bed in the first light of dawn in a room jangling with footsteps, taking in the troublesome news of Mahanam's arrival, Aritra realized that those had not been birds in his dream, but eyes. Someone was coming, had come, and was looking through the eyes of the flying birds. And had gone back. What a strange connection. Was it a coincidence? Or were the beginning, middle and end of the mystery of life always linked together? Mahanam had arrived after eighteen years. And, in those same moments, so had someone else within his dream. Looking through the eyes of the flying birds. *Aadheko ghumey, noyono chumey*. In half-sleep, kissing my eyes.

Aritra was still in a trance. Exhausted, he said regretfully, 'I fell asleep.'

Esha said, 'It's bound to happen. If you're going to be up so late with your poetry and beer, with your beer and poetry, oversleeping is inevitable.'

Ari said, 'Inevitable indeed. I must have been absorbed in something when you left. You went away quietly while I slept—you couldn't have left otherwise. And because you did, you keep returning in my sleep now. Fragmented like a cubist canvas. Sometimes with a terrifying blizzard in your hair, sometimes with a body reaching up to the sky like a eucalyptus pole, sometimes as a bird, as clouds, as water. Why am I confused every time, Esha? Who, what, why, when—a thousand questions raise a storm in my head. Your precious footsteps fly off like dry leaves in this tornado. After they have been lost, long afterwards, my soul realizes you were here and yet you weren't.'

Neelam brought tea. For both of them. A cool early morning breeze blew in through the window. Aritra wrapped himself in the sheet. Accepting a cup, he asked, 'Where's Pupu?'

'Not up yet. I didn't wake her.'

'Why not? It's been so long since all three of us had a cup of tea together.'

Hurt gathered in Neelam's eyes. She said, 'Considering what I just told you, don't you think you and I should first have a talk without Pupu present? Mahanam may turn up any moment.'

Aritra said, 'Don't you know, Neel, that talking about it is pointless? You and I cannot even imagine the direction that Mahanam will attack from. So it's best not to be prepared.'

'What shall we tell Pupu?'

'Pupu is old enough, give her the chance to come to her own conclusions. Only if she asks does the question of answering arise.' He added lightly, 'Don't worry so much. There's nothing to worry about.'

Neelam said, displeased, 'What does it matter to you!' Abruptly she picked up the tea tray and left. Looking at her, Aritra told himself, 'You have to solve your own problem, Neelam. I cannot reject my responsibility, but you must accept yours too. I can stand by you, but the problem of your conscience is yours alone.'

Early March mornings in Pune carried more than a touch of the mountain chill. Kharkibazaar and Priyalkarnagar presented their backs to the south-west monsoon winds. The locals found the mildly cold weather very pleasant. To people from eastern India this kind of cold was positively thrilling. Like a pleasant, soothing caress. It rained frequently, lowering the temperature in one fell swoop. Otherwise, as the day progressed, the sunshine turned golden in the heat of the unpolluted sky. The skin reddened under this sun, even if it did not shine with perspiration, when riding on the scooter from one end of the city to the other, from the suburbs of Pimpri to Priyalkarnagar, from Priyalkarnagar to Shivaji nagar station, through the university, Deccan College, the Chatursbrungi temple, the cantonment and the Pune municipal areas. There was no need for caution. This heat did not lay anyone low. From the bathroom Ari could hear the angry growl of Pupu's scooter. Because Ari was still largely confined to his bed, Pupu was the only one to run errands for her mother. Neelam was so obsessed with the patient and her household that she had no time to go out. Pupu would probably have to do the mid-week shopping for food today, which was why she had left so early. She would bathe when she returned and then go to college. Although Neelam was a competent housewife, she was becoming a little absentminded these days. And very insistent. If Pupu forgot to get something she had asked for, she refused to wait, sending her daughter back to the shops. Pupu was indifferent to all this. She ran the errands mechanically, with no objection to going to the market twice or even thrice in succession. Maybe the scooter gave her the joy of riding a horse. Aritra had bought her the scooter only last year. She used to ride a cycle earlier. It was quite arduous to cycle such long distances. Nor was it particularly healthy for girls to cycle so much. Pupu had been astonished by her birthday gift at first, even forgetting to express her happiness. She had actually scolded her father mildly.

'This is mine? Just for me? Why? We have a car already Baba, you really overdo things sometimes.'

'Not overdoing anything. You can't use the car when I go out. I know you're finding it difficult with the cycle.'

Then Pupu had come running to her father to hug him. Aritra trembled at Pupu's touch. She had grown up now. He was not entitled to such physical affection from her. To assume that he still merited them on the strength of being her father made him anxious, which Neelam did not understand. Or, even if she did, she did not let it be known. However, Pupu was slow, restrained by nature. She seldom allowed herself such wild, childlike spontaneity.

Aritra emerged from the bathroom, pressing his towel to his hair to soak up the water. He had put on his kurta without drying himself properly. The wet spots throbbed in the chilly weather. Peeping in, he found his bedroom had been cleaned thoroughly. A gap in the eastern wall led to a small anteroom, which Ari referred to as the sanctum sanctorum. On the wall of this atom-sized room an eagle held an egg-shaped mahogany rack in its beak. On it rested a few select representatives of Neelam's three hundred and thirty million gods and goddesses. She was devoted to beauty and modesty, therefore Lakshmi. Because of a reputation for being easily-pleased, a Shivling. An image of Durga, slayer of misfortune, and the national god of Maharashtra, Ganapati. The priestess had not combed her hair yet, her broad, fair face was cleansed and tinged with red after a bath, her eyes were tightly shut. Refined, gentle, humble, her sari drawn around her shoulder. Simple arrangements. No incantations, no prayers, just a few grains of cardamom on a silver plate, and, in a silver tumbler, a drop of water collected from the dying canal of the Mulamutha river that ran behind the Ganesh temple. Some flowers deposited at the feet of the idols of Ganesh and Lakshmi. Neelam was performing her puja. Possibly with greater devotion than on other days. Or so it seemed.

There was no point disturbing her now. She would not respond no matter how many times she was called. But Aritra could not wait a moment after his bath. He needed his tea and breakfast at once. Or else his hunger turned into squirming worms in his belly. Neelam knew this. When he was bedridden, she would follow the routine diligently, bringing him his food as soon as she had wiped him down. Ari gazed for some time at Neelam the priestess. When he was a child, toy sellers commonly sold a sort of elongated balloon with a dimpled body, which the children loved. Who knew whether children liked them today? Neelam used to look like that once upon a time. Rounded, smooth, taut. And now she looked the way a balloon does when it is over-inflated, bulging disproportionately. The sharpness of her nose, the edge to her jaws, the exquisite lines at the corners of her eyes, the twist in her lips—all of them seemed to have been dulled.

She wasn't to blame. It had happened after her hysterectomy. The doctor had warned about something like this. It had been difficult for Ari to talk about it because it had been a sensitive subject for a long time. Still, he dropped some hints occasionally. Neelam was not a fool. But what could he do if she pretended not to understand? She didn't even bother to take all the medicines prescribed. They were forced to use injections at times. 'If I'm going to lose what matters, I might as well lose everything. What's the use of holding on?' That's what she would say with wistful eyes. Then she would suddenly come to him at midnight. 'Ari, Ari, I'm frightened. I'm turning cold with fear.' Aritra would say, 'How many times have I told you to take the medicines?' Evening came early. Neelam had turned numb with suffering.

The doctor understood these things. He had said, 'If you let things go on this way, uterine cancer will develop nine times out of ten. What do you want to do?'

'She is only thirty.'

'Which is exactly why I'm asking.'

'What are the after-effects of this operation?'

'Her health will improve remarkably. She will be able to work more, she won't fall ill easily. She may turn into an Amazon.' The doctor hadn't lowered his cigarette from his lips for a long time. 'But.'

'What?' Aritra had asked impatiently.

'She will no longer be a wife.'

'Meaning?'

'Instead, you may get a mother.'

'What do you mean, doctor?'

'Your wife will reach middle age very early, Mr Chowdhury. In her appearance, in her nature. Housewife, mother—these will be appropriate roles for her. She may not be able to play the role of a young woman very well. She will lose interest in that kind of life. In one sense both of you will end your youth with this operation.'

'But I am not ill. I am a full-blown man.' Aritra had jumped out of his chair.

The doctor looked grim. His eyes were sharp, a professional, expert look that bore deep into Aritra Chowdhury's heart. He said, 'That is why. That is why I'm asking. Do you want her life or her youth at this moment? You can't keep both.'

The fundamental truth of Aritra's married life was on the stand. The accuser looked at him with suspicion—at the beating of his heart, at the wails of his soul, his leaping rage, his fears. In a choked voice Aritra said, 'Of course I want her . . . her life. That is the first consideration,' and then, after a pause, 'and also the last.'

The doctor's chamber seemed to have been holding its breath. Now it breathed. The doctor spoke softly, sympathetically, 'But whether it's life or youth, everything is joint property, community property, belonging to both of you, don't you think? Talk to your wife, Mr Chowdhury. Find out what she wants. I'm saying that ninety per cent of cases are dangerous. But that still leaves ten per cent. She could be among them if fortune favours her. What she wants is also very important. Go to her, explain everything.'

Neelam was silent for some time when she heard. Then she said, 'Of course not. There's no question of surgery. I have to take the risk. Forgive me, Ari.'

'But Neelam, you will enter this stage of life in natural course one day or another. It's only a change in the way you live. Isn't that a life too? Perhaps this will open the door to other joys. Why be afraid of it? The alternative to an operation is cancer, do you understand? And unbearable pain, and the end.'

Her voice choking with agony and doubt clouding her eyes, Neelam had replied, 'I don't fear for myself, Ari. I am afraid for you. Of you. What use will I be to you anymore?'

Aritra's face turned white as chalk. What was Neelam saying? Could he trust his ears? Did he deserve such a cruel judgement? Was this verdict his due? Then let me prove, Neelam, that your judgement, your verdict, is completely incorrect. I desired your youth because it was part of your unique self. Neelam was weeping with her head on a bewildered, desperate Ari's chest. She had understood his pain. 'I was wrong, forgive me Ari. I feel desire too.' After a long time, after such a long time Neelam had come to him on her own. When your love comes to you like the rain after a long famine, how extraordinary the madness of those showers is! What a magical honeymoon they spent that night in the room of the blue sky. Just before youth was sacrificed.

It had been a long time but Aritra had not forgotten that night. Perhaps Neelam had. She wanted to forget. Now her eyes were lowered, the end of her sari was draped around her neck, a radiant orbit of uncombed hair around her head. Neelam was deep in worship. Don't disturb her, Aritra. She will tidy up your room all day, arrange flowers, consult a thick pile of books to cook Chinese, Mughlai and Continental food. Aritra didn't have to spend any time on Pupu either—her education, her tennis, her rowing. Nor did he have to take care of the banking, shopping, the mail, social relationships with people in Calcutta—nothing, nothing. Only, Aritra and Neelam now slept in separate rooms.

TWO

Normally Piku and Esha led such uneventful lives that Piku herself felt claustrophobic at times. At nine every morning they took their mini buses from Central Park, one to Dalhousie and the other, to north Calcutta. From one end of the city to the other. Fighting through long traffic jams, taking two to two-and-a-half hours to cover what should have taken one. Tea in the morning, coffee in the evening. Conversations with the coffee pot between them. Reading magazines. Then the desk, pen in hand, notebook on the table, books on the shelves. Sometimes, the typewriter. A head packed with thoughts. A mountain of notebooks, red and blue ball-point pens. Piku would say, 'How can you live like this? Let's go for a film.'

'What film?'

'Who knows? Whatever's running. Give me the newspaper, let's see what's on.'

'Rubbish! Imagine watching a film just for the sake of watching a film! Very tiresome. Find someone else to go with, please, Piku.'

Piku would say, 'You're a bore! You think I have no other friends? Why don't you realize I don't want to leave you alone? Don't you ever wonder why every day has the same colour, Esha? Always a low, slack, off-key note. Why should life be so mundane?'

Esha began to laugh. 'Were you born thinking life is a romance novel? Then no one can prevent heartbreak for you, Piku. If you go for a film blindly you'll be very disappointed.'

'What to do, then?'

'Nothing. Just wait. And that too, not impatiently.'

Piku would say, 'Tchah! I'm off to water the plants then. The yellow hibiscus is budding. Let's see if it's bloomed.'

Esha told herself, 'Well spotted, Piku. So ordinary and yet so extraordinary. Hibiscus, but a yellow one—as you watch the moments bloom, forget the grandeur you're anticipating. If it comes, it will come. And no harm done if it doesn't.'

This was how the days passed, the months too—they were spent ripping out the pages of the calendar and tossing them in the dustbin. Piku went for films, to picnics with friends, spent three days at her niece's birthday party instead of a single evening, and came back refreshed. She fell in love anew with their home in Central Park, the veranda, the garden, the conversations, the unlit nights on the terrace with the door locked and mats laid out, stars and glow-worms, glow-worms and stars, the sweet fragrance of flowers, humming, sleep. You're so strange, Esha. You could have gone on the excursion. Didn't you get a wedding invitation the other day, why didn't you go? Not in the mood. I like it this way, I really do. Then, at mid-morning, a potter's wheel began to whirl in her head suddenly. A bird flapped its wings in her breast, pecking on her lymph nodes with its restless beak. Fluids began to drain out of the cage of her body, the currents seeking release. Esha felt like dying if she couldn't go away somewhere at these times. She realized clearly that she had already been reborn and re-reborn. It wasn't only cowards who died many times before their death. Even those who live on intense hope and experiences died and were reborn in the same lifetime. On these occasions Esha realized that here present existence had died. Until she was born again, she would live like a floating spirit.

Everyone had warned her not to take the Geetanjali Express. Although a shorter journey, it meant being on the train during the daylight hours of two whole days. Summer had just arrived. A hot wind usually sprang up as soon as the train left Bengal. But there was not an inch of space on the Bombay Mail. Not even the VIP quota worked. A taxi from the booking counters at Fairley Place to Esplanade. Esha was too excited to lean back in her seat. Only after she had got a ticket on the Geetanjali Express did the potter's wheel in her head stop. Crossing space would mean traversing time, the inability to do which had always made humans sad. This urge within her to go away was a fundamental one. When it came, an image kept playing in her head, telling her where she should go. A dream on a full-moon night of a eucalyptus-lined avenue and a pair of siris trees arched over the road had led her to Rikhia. A vision of an expanse of cracked red earth fading in the distance under the sun had taken her to Daltonganj. The view through a glass window of unrestricted, unending blue Himalayan ranges had brought her to Ranikhet. Images seen in daydreams did not have shadows like night-time dreams. Sometimes these images were a blinding Van Gogh painting under a real sun, yellow fireworks on real mustard fields, or Jatin Sengupta canvases of real rivers tilting around one sharp curve after another. They made her twist in intense pain. Esha would take the image out of her heart and put it in her lap, hold it in her arms again, and finally hear a little boy crying like the high-pitched whistle of a train. Trembling with a fever in her passion for distant places, she kept saying, what do I do, I have no leave from the office, I have spent all my money building my house, and yet I'm drawn irresistibly to a Bhutia tea picker with a sweet, scrubbed face and a wicker basket on her back, working on a harsh but beautiful mountain plateau while the golden dust from cows' hooves rises in the air, drawing me like a mother does, like the breeze on a spring night does, like a lover. I must go. Or else I will ignore Piku when she conjures up a new glow with fragrant golden tea in brand-new pink cups and saucers. I shall walk in the garden reluctantly, perhaps the flowers will say good morning, I shall be distracted and ignore them. The December dahlias bent over with pain, the first flowers of monsoon, the gentle melody of the jasmine vines on the lintel—I won't allow them near me, I shall go deep into my pyre, deeper, while the beads of khoi are scattered on the road with cruel indifference during the final journey.

I shan't care for their pain. It's not as though anyone has cared for mine. I shall spend hours in the shower, Piku will be fed up of calling me. I will take my clothes from the hangars arranged by Piku in my wardrobe and put them on mechanically. I shan't remember whether I'm going out or have just come in. Piku will say, 'Aren't you eating?' It's not as if it will make any difference whether I eat or not. There were no elaborate meals anymore, no one threw away the leftovers in the back lane after a night of celebration. Now a meal was only a response to hunger. Whatever was available. Bread and butter, boiled potato and rice, sweetened peanuts, anything.

This time the image that came to her was related to food. As she was leafing through the Unesco album on Ajanta and Ellora, sleep descended on her eyes. Esha saw an embodiment of grief in the form of Krishna, alone in a chamber. Nothing but shadows in the room. A friend brings in a plate of rare delicacies and a plea in her eyes. The young woman is stilled, unmoving, her sadness beyond explanation. Once, twice, thrice, the image knocked on her mind and came back. At dawn a butterfly had flown in to perch, trembling, on the curtain drawn across the southern window. A bird that didn't know how to sing—or had forgotten—chirped sleepily on a branch outside—tiktik, tuktuk, tiktik, tuktuk. Her hair, which she had not tied up the previous evening, was spread across her back and shoulders, her hands linked on her knees. Piku stared at her in surprise. Esha said, 'I'm going to Ajanta, Piku, I want to see Ajanta.'

'This very moment?' said Piku. 'Go, then.'

Her eyes were on the wall. Esha said with a gentle smile, 'I have felt this way before. Manasa madhuram. A beautiful notion. But I want to go like Yudhisthir when he wanted to ascend to heaven with his body intact.'

'Your companions on the journey will fall dead one by one.'

'Let them. I'm not taking you lest you become one of them.'

'Going with a dog?'

Mukhia was barking in the veranda. It was this sound that probably made Piku think of the dog.

Esha said, 'Mukhi is all yours. You know that very well. I have given him to you as a gift. I give him a bath and food sometimes because you're scattered about his care. That doesn't mean your Mukhi will follow me.'

'Don't you know you cannot enter heaven without a dog!'

'That's a street dog. It follows at a distance, doesn't brush its tail against you, doesn't lick you everywhere like you're a stick of ice cream, certainly doesn't nag.'

'There's also that whole business of visiting hell.'

'Look Piku, those who have been visiting hell in different ways all their life should not object to another visit in order to go to heaven.'

'You'll find Duryodhan and the rest of them sitting on thrones along with their courtiers, don't forget.'

'Now you're really making me worry. Never mind all that. I'm definitely going. The last time was with my uncle and aunt when I was twelve. The porter carried our luggage across an empty field, the three of us were to spend the night at a government bungalow in Fardapur. My uncle told us that Ajanta was discovered in several stages, that there were probably tigers hereabouts at the time. And we were going to see it all in a single day. I still remember how the Bagoda river twists and turns. See, just like Ceres's call to Proserpine at the end of the year, Ajanta's call has reached me here in Hades.'

'What! How can you refer to our home as Hades!'

'You know perfectly well I can't possibly refer to our home as Hades. Only if my heart is weighed down even in a paradise of pleasure will I use that name. I can scale any peak to escape this horrible mood, the altitude of Ajanta is nothing in comparison. But visiting a new place won't do, I have to go with a new heart, a different state of mind.'

'Take care as you go,' said Piku.

From the booking office Esha went directly to the Esplanade post office and despatched a telegram. REACHING KALYAN BY GEETANJALI, MARCH 17. The west coast was completely unknown to her. Except Bombay. She knew no one else. Going alone to Lucknow had proved to be a terrible experience. She had no idea there were so many Romeos in Lucknow. A hippie was wandering about right next to her in patchwork clothes with a rucksack on her back and a camera in her hand, but no one disturbed her. But an Indian woman in a sari must not travel alone. What did the descendants of Shivaji's Mavli soldiers do for a living now? What if no one was waiting for her at Kalyan? She would have to take the connecting train to Pune alone. Who knew how late she would reach. But then there was bound to be a retiring room. She would spend the night there and find the tourist office in the morning. To Ajanta via Aurangabad.

Esha did not know why she had sent a telegram to Aritra Chowdhury. He should have been the first among the last people on Earth whom Esha could wire. And yet this occurred to her only after she had sent the telegram. Esha bit her lip with her teeth. She did not know what had made her do this. Her entire life was a perfect progress report of her penchant for burying all her natural proclivities under a rock. Sometimes these aborted wishes took revenge. Leaving the post office and walking towards the bus depot, Esha felt that occasional defeats like these were healthy. Small defeats. Large victories.

The hesitant telegram reached its destination with several hops, like a chick that had just learnt to fly. It had been sent to Aritra's office address. He had not joined yet. So Mandal, his personal assistant, delivered it at home riding his scooter at breakneck speed. Aritra was sitting with Neelam in a patch of sun on their tiny lawn, having his afternoon tea. Neelam had made pastries today. Chocolate cream. Pupu had taken a box on her trip to Goa with friends, for eating on the train. Putting the telegram down on the table, Mandal clicked his heels and saluted in military style, saying, 'I don't have a minute today, Bhabi. Keep my pastry for some other time. You won't forget, I hope.'

Smiling, Neelam said, 'Do you have more telegrams to distribute? Have you been demoted now that your boss is out of action?'

Mandal said, 'Sweet are the uses of demotion if it makes

me arrive at people's homes in time for evening tea. But it isn't that, Bhabi. We're expecting guests from my wife's family at home, if I'm late I'll be skinned alive.'

'How dare you blame your wife? Run along at once.'

Mandal turned and leapt on to his scooter, disappearing instantly in a cloud of dust. He always received a warm welcome here. Not just him. Neelam Bhabi was the centre of attraction for a large squad of Lakshmans. Her influence on them was much higher than Aritra's. One of Neelam's greatest qualities was that she did not take hierarchy into consideration. She was as warm with the personal assistant as with the chief engineer—they attracted her as human beings. This attitude was not easy to come by in any industrial area. Of course, the workers in Pune's industrial outfits lived all over the city. There was no industrial colony here like Tatanagar or IIT Colony. So some of the characteristics of a large metropolis were visible here. It was hard to say whether Neelam's natural democratic ways would have survived otherwise.

Priyalkarnagar had been built from scratch. There was still white dust everywhere. It made things dusty, but not dirty. Tall trees lined both sides of the road a little further ahead. There were plenty of bushes around the blocks of buildings. High fences had been put up now. Mandal turned into a dot amidst the trees and disappeared. Neelam said, 'Is everything all right at home? What's the matter? What is it?' Aritra had dropped the telegram as though it was a scorpion. 'Esha is coming. Seventeenth March. Geetanjali.'

Neelam's face competed with Aritra's in turning ashen.

She couldn't speak, and went away a little later, her tea half drunk. Ari remained sitting with his own cup. Why had he reacted this way? No matter what Neelam might feel, was this telegram really unexpected? The essence of the letters he had sent day after day from his revolving chair set on the light green tiles of a room painted in pastel shades of green and pink acrylic was: Come, Esha. Come and see for yourself. The tree of the world grows in silence, not on love or the lack of it. The leaves, the flowers, the green canopy of this silent tree provides refuge, believe me. Come, Esha. A bed of the ashes of humiliation does not befit you. Then why shouldn't Esha telegram him? Aritra was not a liar! Was he destined to be a liar in Esha's eyes all his life? And yet all his other relationships were ticking along just like a well-oiled clock. Was his relationship with only one person a lie? He did not tell her what he wanted. Ari would ask Esha, 'Why did you come Esha?' Esha would say, 'But you wanted me to.'

Would Ari confess then: 'I didn't mean it.'

Or was the Aritra who had a relationship with Esha actually another Aritra within himself, whom he was only half familiar with? He could not understand this Aritra. Ari stood up, his face drawn, and went into the house, dragging his foot a little. Neelam was sitting on a divan in the drawing room, a coconut tree and the bright sea of Anjuna near her head. A jagged coastline. A few hippies were visible indistinctly in the poster running the width of the room. Beneath the ecstatic Anjuna beach Neelam's misery was absolutely flesh-and-blood, real. Corporeal.

'What's the matter?' said Aritra.

Neelam didn't answer.

When she saw Aritra standing the same way much later, his face stricken, she said, 'When did you ask her to come? Was it as soon as you regained consciousness after the operation? Did you dictate the letter to Mandal? Your personal assistant.'

Aritra was stunned. 'Why should I have asked her to come?'

'It's natural to think of your loved ones when you think of death.'

Aritra said gravely, 'I didn't ask Esha to come, Neelam. I did write casually once or twice asking her to visit. But not in the recent past. I write to her from time to time. You can read the letters if you like. I don't know why she wants to come. If it bothers you very much, I'd better telegram her expressing our inability.'

'No need,' Neelam answered briefly and left the room.

THREE

Mahanam could have stayed at the Film Institute if he had wanted to. As a guest. Arrangements had been made. But Chandrashekhar had said, 'You have such a busy programme, Dr Roy. It won't be convenient to stay there. Are you afraid because I have a bachelor establishment? Just try my cooking. A few days with you would also dispel my loneliness temporarily.'

When Chandrashekhar went to Calcutta he usually accepted Mahanam's hospitality. One library, two readers. With Yagneshwar looking after both of them. Not that there was anyone like Yagneshwar here, which Chandrashekhar had no problem with. He had spent several years abroad. Cooking for himself had become a habit. Every morning he made Mahanam two large sandwiches, served with sauce, a banana and an enormous glass of coffee with milk. Lunch was at Max Mueller Bhavan for the first few days. The lecture course ended on Tuesday—after a day's gap on Wednesday, the film institute seminar would start on Thursday.

Mahanam enjoyed such packed schedules. He wouldn't even have minded had there been no hyphen on Wednesday. He had incredible strength—of body, of mind, of intelligence—which he had not had the opportunity to make good use of. His entire life seemed to have passed in play. Playing with dust and earth. There must have been a playful personality within him, propelling him all the time. When he tried to estimate his real achievements, this role-play became clear. That apart, Mahanam was happy. The fewer occasions he had to brood, the more he enjoyed things. On Thursday Chandrashekhar took him for a kulfi after returning from the university. It was a favourite of Mahanam's. As he ate he said, 'You know, Chandrashekhar, when I observe my own excessive gratification from food, I sometimes feel I am still at what you call the oral sucking stage. Oral sucking, oral biting—don't you have all these bizarre things?'

Chandrashekhar said with a smile, 'You would not have been so independent in that case. But you are, aren't you?'

'Not at all. I depend entirely on Yagneshwar in Calcutta. Here too, see how easily I accepted your invitation. If I'd stayed elsewhere I'd have had to take my own responsibility to some extent at least.'

'You're doing it here too. You're washing your own underclothes. Doing the breakfast dishes. Making tea for me in the evening.'

'But see how casual I am. Never took anything in life seriously. Que sera, sera. This isn't the sign of a mature person.'

Chandrashekhar said, 'You never thought about yourself so much before, what's happened?'

'Must be post-forty depression. Been going on for quite some time.' Mahanam helped himself to another pistachio kulfi. The taste of condensed milk, green with pistachios. It looked lovely too. Turning it round and round in his hand like a Japanese cup and looking closely at it, Mahanam put his plate down. 'What you eat must also look gorgeous, Shekhar. Look at this kulfi—as pretty as a costumed dancer.'

'Just that she has barely got on stage when her act ends,' said Chandrashekhar.

'My entire life has passed in such brief enjoyment, Shekhar.'

'Somehow you are caught up in the indulgence of nothing-achieved-in-my-life today.'

'If Tagore himself could say even after all his poetry, novels, short stories, plays, songs, folk art, university and cultural tours, even an agricultural bank, how little I have achieved, what are people like us supposed to say?'

'Look at it from another perspective. Those who get this feeling are on a quest for perfection that is higher than anyone else's. Isn't that so?'

'Rubbish. Do you get this feeling too?'

'Not at all. Every evening I pat myself on the back, oh, you've done so much work today. I'm leaving a mark on this earth.'

Chandrashekhar began to laugh loudly. 'I even demand extra praise from society and the world because I cook for myself.'

'You can certainly do that, Shekhar. You're a top-class chef.'

'My sandwiches tell you what a good cook I am?'

'Back where I live they say those who can make tea and paan well are inevitably good cooks. Since you wield the sandwich like paan, therefore . . .'

'What did you say? I wield the sandwich like paan?'

'Of course. Whenever we meet you hand me a sandwich, you're forever chewing on one, and you make me do the same. I am sure your culinary skills produce a gourmet repast at night, but by then I have no appetite left.'

Chandrashekhar burst out laughing.

'If only you'd told me earlier. After all those years abroad I've become so used to sandwiches and hot dogs and hamburgers that . . . Why didn't you tell me this food doesn't suit you?'

'I would have if it didn't.' Mahanam smiled. 'You've taken me back to my student days—in other words, to my first youth—through food alone. How can it not suit me? Have you noticed that every memory has a smell attached to it? There's a sauce you add to your ham sandwich, Worcester sauce, possibly, I don't taste it so much as I immerse myself in it, and around me there are seven- or eight-hundred-year-old red brick houses—fireplaces, chimneys, professors with white manes, dapper dons, rose gardens with the scent of English grass. Lanes overflowing with tradition. Trinity College, Christ Church, Magdalene, Pembroke, Queen's.'

'Is the most delicious time of life necessarily in the past? I can't accept that.'

'Only in the past? I won't say that. But just like the Gujaratis who start their meal with a sweet dish, we start life the same away. Bitter, pungent, spicy, hot, dry—all these flavours come later. It's a bit like starting with rasgullas, going on to biryani, and ending with neem-begun—bitter vegetables.'

'What on earth is neem-begun?'

'You've had it at my house, you've forgotten entirely. Neem leaves—margosa. Crisply fried and served with small aubergine fritters.'

'Oh my god it was incredibly bitter.'

'That's because you haven't acquired the taste. Coffee, cheese—these things have a pungent flavour too, many people don't like them at first, but they swear by them afterwards. Our Bengali margosa with aubergine is the same. Besides, it has many qualities. It's an excellent appetizer.'

'In that case why finish the meal with the appetizer?'

'What do you mean "why". Meals always begin with appetizers, but in the case of life, the bitter part comes at the end, when it tastes good, excellent, in fact. If you've ever observed old men you'll know what I mean. Everything tastes bitter, they claim. Followed by: is that phuchka you're having, let me taste a couple.'

'You mean the taste of life has been concentrated on the lips and tongue. The oral sucking stage.'

'The oral sucking stage. Yes. The daughter-in-law's a mother by then, the daughter too, but if they pay attention to anyone else you start pouting.'

'How did you learn all this? At home it's just been Yagneshwar and you.'

'You think my stock of second-hand experiences is meagre? Nothing escapes my eye, Shekhar.'

They were very late getting back home. Mahanam had scoured Pune Camp in his auto-taxi. Dazzling lights at the garden by the dam, which Shekhar had suggested he take a look at. 'No gardens or arbours now,' said Mahanam. 'I'm only trying to sense the city, Shekhar. But despite several hundred years of history your Pune hasn't really developed a personality or a character. The Peshwas' Poona and the modern industrial Poona have not blended. This city is probably the greatest example of the fact that wide roads, shopping complexes, homes, colleges, universities and parks alone do not a vibrant city make.'

'Those who live here feel very cramped in other cities though. So much space.'

'You're right. Space. Only space. Without support. Maybe this is my Calcutta sensibility. But even if you put aside big cities like Bombay and Delhi and Madras, even places like Bangalore or Ahmedabad or Chandigarh seem to have clear identities. I'm told our famous romantic writer Sharadindu Bandyopadhyay used to live here. Do you know of him?'

'Uh-huh,' said Chandrashekhar.

Chandrashekhar lived in a single-storey building with a beautiful personal lawn. Besides a garden shared with the other flats. Two bedrooms, one of which he had turned into a study. Mahanam had picked this room. The smell of books was good for sleep. When it was past eleven at night Chandrashekhar put a sheet over Mahanam, who was sitting in silence in the lawn. Conversation, then more conversation, after which they lapsed into silence. Much later Mahanam said, 'The past has been preserved as a museum in your Pune, the present doesn't seem to exist either, only the future. But there's something that's very beautiful.'

'What?'

'Blue nights. Bluish mornings. Your Pimpri has shown me exactly what poets mean by such phrases.'

'Explain.'

'All the houses in this satellite town of yours are new. Planned suburbs. Well spread out. Nothing coming in the way of the eye. Wherever you look, a unified blue sky. At night, even when these sights all around us are sunk in darkness, it feels as though we're sitting inside a covered blue tent. Quite literally a blue night. And then the same thing in the morning, though a little different. There's still no mist, and even if there is, the sky has lowered itself to surround us on all sides in a way that makes the elevation of these houses and trees quite insignificant.'

Chandrashekhar said, 'So when poets talk of violet moons or maroon lights, we have to consider all of them true?'

'True? Of course. Completely real, concrete, corporeal. When the moon rises on the night of Holi in Shantiniketan, it is glittering white. We're used to a red moon. We cannot even imagine the full moon being white. Actually the less dust there is in the atmosphere, the cleaner the moon looks.

The violet moon is also thanks to the play of those dust particles, the maroon light too. It all depends on the angle at which the rays of the sun fall. Of course, that doesn't mean poets don't resort to rhetoric or imagination. I'm just trying to remind you that much of the experiences of poets is real.'

'So when the poet writes, when the evening is spread out against the sky, like a patient etherized upon a table, that's a concrete affair too?'

'What do you mean? This is just a metaphor. Which is being used to convey the usual mood of the scene and its effect on the viewer. This is quite different.'

Abashed, Chandrashekhar said, 'Actually you recite poetry so well, Dr Roy, that my interest grows. We are used to seeing any work of art as a sublimation of the id, or some kind of explosion of a knowledge-less state, or some sort of defence mechanism. We are not trained to appreciate the beauty of poetry objectively. Something strange happens to me when you read. I no longer remember having studied psychology.'

'Not just psychology, Chandrashekhar, you should not remember having studied anything at all. A pleasurable experience only uses the edge of our perception. At that point we become beings of sensation and solitude. Later we return to being our educated, cultured, restrained, social selves, where memory acts as a vital controller. Actually it is you psychologists who should tell us exactly what takes place when we enjoy art. I am trespassing.'

'Not at all. As someone who enjoys art you can see the direct aspect of the experience. And as a theorist you are analysing the reasons behind it. None of this is trespassing.'

Suddenly Mahanam said, 'By the way Chandrashekhar, do you know Aritra Chowdhury? Used to live in old Pune earlier. These days I think . . .'

Chandrashekhar said, 'Aritra Chowdhury, chief public relations officer of JPJ Industries? Is there anyone who doesn't know him? He's the pillar of the Bengali community. Puja celebrations, concerts, poetry conferences. He's very enthusiastic about all this. So is his wife. It's thanks to them we've got to know all of Tagore's dance drama productions thoroughly. You never told me you knew him.'

'No, I didn't. But some old scores . . . wer . . . weren't you saying I should see everything here minutely in order to strengthen the cultural unity between Maharashtra and West Bengal? To do that, the first item on my list should be Aritra Chowdhury.'

'Why, exactly? Is it because he publicizes Bengali culture in Maharashtra? Did you know that?'

'No no,' Mahanam laughed. 'He has a very interesting history.'

'What is it? Is he some sort of exhibit?'

'Certainly an exhibit. Poet-turned-executive, Bohemian-turned-householder, a rebel tamed by silver.'

Chandrashekhar said in astonishment, 'I smell something mysterious. Is he an old friend of yours? He seems a little younger.'

'After a certain age young and old, master and pupil, father and son—they're all one Shekhar; you don't seem to have reached that age yet.'

'I don't know,' said Shekhar, 'I have the mind of an

Indian, after all. There's always a fear of losing respect. Ever since I met you for the first time at Cornell, a conviction that you're an elder statesman has taken root in me.'

'This is not a compliment at all, Shekhar. I have never been in favour of considering myself younger or older than anyone else. It makes communication difficult. Besides, you mustn't revere time so much, it takes advantage of you. I prefer to be eternally thirty-nine. If I turn forty I fear I'll become a scoundrel like Shaw.'

Chandrashekhar was laughing. Mahanam said, 'Your friend who picked me up from the station knows Aritra Chowdhury's house. I dropped by on the day I came here. Went out of my way. Can you telephone your friend and see if he's available?'

'No need,' said Chandrashekhar. 'My car was sent for servicing, it'll be back tomorrow. Either Khar or west Priyalkarnagar. I can take it out.'

'No,' said Mahanam.

'But why? It's no problem.'

'Not for you maybe, but it is for me.' Mahanam smiled mysteriously. 'I'm going alone.'

Mahanam was stuffing his pipe with tobacco absent-mindedly. He was now in the veranda with the black-and-white marble pattern in his Duff Street home, talking to the young research scholar from the university who had come with a letter of introduction from Dr Sadhu. It was his third visit. This time he was accompanied by a girl. There was an areca palm in an enormous brass pot on Mahanam's right. On the left a stone figure of a boy was engaged in playing with a heavy ball. This scene, this meeting, and the subsequent conversation would be repeated many times. The young man was restless, intelligent and stubborn. Mahanam could not make out what the young woman with him was like.

FOUR

Neelam usually woke up quite early. She used the services of a maid and a cleaner, whom she supervised constantly, standing by with her hands on her hips as they worked. What remained to be done afterwards was still by no means inconsiderable. Ari and Pupu called it her mania. From cleaning the bathroom to tidying the kitchen, Neelam did it all with her own hands. There was never dust or grime here in any case, but on top of this, Neelam's obsession or cleanliness—whatever it was—ensured that all the corners were perfectly swept, dusted and scrubbed. Even when she cooked, Neelam kept two or three different kinds of dusters within reach. The oil and spices weren't allowed to leave the tiniest of stains on the tiles. Not even on the rims or corners of the bowls. And definitely not on her hands. Ari said she cooked like they did in TV commercials. Today Neelam was already done with her bath and puja. The fragrance of flowers and, stronger still, the scent of incense had percolated into her sleeping husband's slumber. Neelam normally drank her first cup of tea without getting out of her nightdress. It was only today that she had bathed early and was standing by Ari's bed, bringing with her a whiff of lotuses. It was a special day. Ari would be going to office today after three months. Although the doctor had approved another spell of long leave in a few days.

When Ari saw Neelam looking so tenderly at him, his heart overflowed with impossible joy. The feeling was linked to his childhood and his memories of his mother. Man or woman, everyone wants to go back to their mother all their life. They admit as much to at least one person, to themselves too. But these unprovoked little pleasures are unfailing indicators of the eternal bond with one's mother.

'How come a village belle has brought me my morning tea?' asked Ari. 'What's going on?'

'What! Have you forgotten it's a special day?' Neelam frowned.

Ari groped around in his memory desperately. He felt as though he were playing blind-man's bluff. Wedding anniversary? No, that was in October. Pupu's birthday? The searing heat of June. Ari's own birthday was in December, an occasion for Neelam to throw a grand party every year. Was it Neelam's birthday, then? As far as he could remember, it was in February or something. He couldn't be sure. Summoning an enigmatic expression to his face, Ari said, 'Forgotten! So easily? 'Tis thy birthday. Presently on the journey to life . . .'

'Oh my god, is that what you think?' said Neelam. 'You've forgotten my birthday, and now you're pretending to remember. Shame on you.'

'Well then stop blaming me,' smiled Ari. 'Please tell me what's so special today.'

'You're rejoining work today. Don't tell me you forgot.'

'Oh, so all this is because I'll be earning again,' exclaimed Aritra in disappointment. 'All these rituals are to celebrate the fact that I'm not going to be dependent on you as a cripple and am taking up the plough once more. That is why my housemate's body is so fragrant today.'

Raising a cloud of talcum powder, Neelam sat down on a chair, avoiding physical contact. Gravely she said, 'Not because you're going to earn again, but because you're returning to a normal, healthy existence. I don't need you to earn for my security, do I? The house is registered in my name. You can't throw me out even if you want to. You don't even know where the documents are. On the contrary, I can get you into trouble if I want to. Better not take a chance.'

Aritra stared at her in mock dismay. 'You mean I've made so many mistakes at the same time? It's a calamity! I'll obviously have to be very wary of you from now on.'

Sipping her tea, Neelam pursed her lips. 'As if you're going to be wary of me ever. Anyway, that's up to you. I've sent a telegram to Bikram.'

Aritra seemed to have been administered an electric shock.

'Whatever for?'

'I've asked them to come. Around the twentieth of March.'

A perplexed Aritra said after a long gap, 'So you're playing on the front foot?'

'The back foot isn't good enough anymore. And besides, why take it that way? I'm sure Esha isn't coming just to meet you or me, she's coming because she wants to travel. Given the state you're in, who will go with her? I've organized travelling companions for her. Thank me.'

'Let me tell you something, Neelam,' declared Aritra. 'If Esha comes, if she really does come, I will never let her alone with Bikram. And besides, I'm quite fit now. If you can't trust me, if you're so afraid, I can wire Esha not to come.'

'But Bikram is coming with his wife. What are you worried about? There's no question of letting her alone with him.'

'Bikram is a terror with or without his wife. No barrier is sufficient to stop him from fulfilling his urges. You know that very well. Tell me, Neelam, isn't Esha a friend of yours too? How could you have considered Bikram a companion for her?'

Neelam answered grimly, 'I don't know, I thought Esha was an adult just as I am. Even if she is still a helpless, powerless, virginal girl in your head, reality says otherwise.'

'I never left you alone with Bikram, Neelam,' said Aritra. 'You were an adult too.'

'An adult, and a young woman of twenty-eight. It still isn't clear to me whether it was Bikram or me that you were afraid of.'

'It seems there's a great deal that's not clear to me either,' said Aritra.

'You don't know these things because you never considered it necessary to know them, Ari. Once a woman is married, no matter how torrid the romance might have been, she is considered married for life. A well-thumbed book, a familiar story, a conquered kingdom—no man tries to understand her further, does he? But he always feels the need to tighten the patrolling. Since that particular need has ended, you probably believe you can do as you please.'

'Patrol whom? What are you referring to as a need that's ended, Neelam?' Irritation was mingled with resentment in Aritra's voice. His first cup of tea had turned cold by now. Gently he said, 'What you're thinking, what you usually think, is distorted perception. If I had wanted to do as I please, you think I couldn't have by now?'

'How do I know whether you have or not?' Neelam's voice had risen a notch, drowning the sound of Pupu's scooter. Aritra lit a cigarette. Pupu entered with the telegram a little later. It had been lying under the music system in the living room ever since it had arrived. It must have fluttered into Pupu's hands today.

'Ma, Baba, who's Esha Khan? The one who's visiting us?'

'Your father's girlfriend,' said Neelam with a smile.

Rising to his feet and stretching, Ari added, 'Your mother's, too.'

'How interesting.' Uttering just two words, Pupu went off to her room. Making what she could of her parents' explanations, she would probably fill up the blanks with her own judgement and imagination.

She emerged soon afterwards, dressed in the baggy clothes she wore at home, drying her hands on a towel. Drops of water shone on her face. With an innocent smile, she said, 'No problem—we can lay out the folding cot in my room.'

Ari did not know how much Pupu had matured. She probably imagined that, despite her father's fondness for his friends, he found it both difficult and troublesome to let go of his privacy, even if it was only for a few days. So she had unhesitatingly relinquished her own rights. Virtually sacrificed them. The major part of their 1,000-square foot flat had been gobbled up by the living room. Two bathrooms had been carved out of the remaining space. A generous kitchen. A balcony, and the portico outside. The two rooms were not very large. The smaller one was under Aritra's control. As for the larger one, Pupu referred to it as her mother's, while her mother referred to it as hers. Neelam slept on the same wide bed as Pupu. Only during the time Ari was fighting with death had she spent a few nights in his room. Since then the poor thing had had to divide her time between the two rooms, looking in on Ari at least twice each night. Neelam could not relax. Sometimes Pupu looked in on her father too.

Neelam stood up. She would give Pupu breakfast now. Pupu ate the heaviest meal of her day at this time. Neelam usually made some dry mutton or chicken or vegetables the previous night. Now she would make fresh parathas—methi paratha or aloo paratha. Pupu would eat heartily, with salad and pickles on the side, and, before going to college, just a glass of milk. Lunch was a fruit or two. Rarely did she take a packed lunch from home. She would shut the door to her room now, and become engrossed in her T-square, set squares, white sheets of paper and diagrams. Not all of this drafting was for her college course. She was obsessed. She had books sent to her from different countries—she wanted to design new housing complexes, new towns. The room had to be left to her entirely sometimes.

Aritra would bathe and leave for office after Pupu had eaten and withdrawn into her room. They could never spend their mornings together. After the father and daughter had left, Neelam would arm herself for battle. Somebody had been studying in this room or had bathed in that bathroom, someone else had been sitting here or lying down there—she wouldn't leave a single sign of their activities, she'd turn the house into a movie set. The maid might be dusting and scrubbing in the bedroom when Neelam's heart would suddenly leap into her mouth in the kitchen. 'Have you wiped the sides of the bed, Bai? The window sills? What's that stain like South America on the window pane? Clean it at once. Use some more detergent—yes, that's better.'

There was plenty of time. But still Aritra sat down to eat as he had bathed already. Neelam was eating too. She put the coffee pot down, arranged the food on the table, and said softly, 'One point. Pupu's suggestion was her own. It doesn't mean we have to do it her away. If Esha comes—why if?—she WILL come—I'm going to sleep in your room. The bed's narrow, but that's all right.'

Ari was eating absently. 'You could sleep in my room even without Esha visiting us,' he said. 'Only you know why you don't.'

'I forgot dessert,' said Neelam. 'I'll be back in a minute.'

She went off to the kitchen without answering—avoiding the question, in other words. She would take the dessert out of the fridge now. Put it in a bowl of warm water to thaw it. Meanwhile Ari would indeed keep eating, but the food on Neelam's plate would turn dry. This was her usual way.

Aritra wondered whether Neelam wanted to keep him under watch. One of the biggest flaws of their home was the lack of a guest room. It was essential for those who lived away from their hometown to have one. The arrival of a guest turned the regular routine upside down, which Aritra did not like at all. He found it difficult to locate the things he needed. Not being able to occupy his usual spots in the house disturbed him constantly. But this was inevitable when they had a guest. The three of them had become used to it. This time too he could have given his room to Esha for a few days and occupied the living room, sleeping on the sofa-cum-bed. Laying out his possessions on the table on which the stereo was kept and in the drawers would not have violated his principles. But under Neelam's arrangements Esha wouldn't have a room to herself, as any guest should if possible. It was different for close friends and regular visitors, but Esha was quite new. She did not know this Aritra, this Neelam, their joint household and, especially, Pupu. Asking her to stay in Pupu's room . . . Who knew what Esha's own habits were like? And yet proposing anything else would lead to misunderstanding and domestic strife—there had never been such conflicts in Aritra's home since Bikram and his wife had left Pune. It was best to accept the suggestions without the slightest protest.

Let Esha come, no matter how, no matter what the sleeping arrangements were. Let Esha come close to him. Once the air in the house had touched Esha, it was certain to touch him too, even if it passed into every room. Ari's home would acquire the boquet of Esha's presence. His marriage would finally be stamped with the seal of acknowledgement. Because Esha would visit, because Esha would touch, because Esha would stay.

Aritra suddenly felt a jolt. What was his relationship with Esha? Was there any justification for considering Esha's acknowledgement the most important and the most absolute? Their earlier relationship certainly did not exist anymore. It had actually acquired a rather complicated form. Whichever city Aritra lived in or had moved to, he had always written to Esha at her old address once or twice a year. And on New Year and Durga Puja, of course. None of them had been answered. Not one. Every time he had posted a letter to her, it had been like leaving flowers on her doorstep. One day after another had passed in the grip of meaninglessness. And then had come the forgetting, amidst work-duty-domesticity-treatment-routine. Forgetting that he was supposed to have got something, but had not. But something within what has been forgotten stirs the currents of blood unknowingly. Someone's blue sari draped itself over the spring sky now. The faint scent of a particular woman wafted in from the leaves on either side of the tree-lined avenues of Priyalkarnagar, making him melancholy. The Sahyadri remained sullen throughout July. Under the buffeting monsoon winds, light and shade glittered—

dusty but radiant, as though the sun shone behind it. Not remembering the luminous delicateness of Esha's skin in the moist rainy season did not mean forgetting it entirely.

But eighteen years afterwards! How was Esha now after eighteen years? What was she like? Two more years and it would have been Jibanananda Das's famous twenty years. The dew had hunted her down. But what if I found you in the mist twenty years later.

After all this time, having ignored an average of two letters a year and therefore thirty-six in all, why had she remembered Aritra? There was a time when Esha would turn to Aritra whenever she was in trouble. These difficult periods were very important to Esha. And a matter of amusement for Aritra. He still found it funny when he thought of it.

Esha had left her diary on the tram. All her secrets were in it. Suddenly there was a telephone call for her at home—Esha's sister-in-law handed the phone to her. Esha took the receiver. 'Hello, may I speak to Miss Tagore please.'

'Miss Tagore? There's no one here named Miss Tagore.'

'No one? Who're you trying to fool? Who's going to write all this poetry except someone from the Tagore family?'

Esha ran to Aritra.

'Ari-da, Ari-da, those horrible fellows are phoning every day. Even though Boudi keeps disconnecting. It's creating a lot of trouble at home. They can even disguise their voices. The diary has not just poems, it has heaps of quotations, they're going to be obscene about them, lots of addresses and phone numbers, they'll annoy everyone.'

Ari listened gravely, doodling.

'Do something, Aritra-da, say something.'

'What can I say? Scatterbrained girls deserve such things. I've told you many times that your diary is not the appropriate place to practise your rhymes.' Apparently all her poetry came to her from the sky. Esha turned away, she was leaving now, a memorable image. Had she come straight out of the Vaishnav Padavali? Her face half obscured by her ever so slightly reddish hair. Eyelids visible. Long lashes. The tip of her nose was shining. Flaring nostrils.

Ari said, 'Listen, Esha, listen. When they telephone again tell them to meet you at the east gate of Victoria Memorial, the gate near Cathedral Road.'

'What rubbish is all this? I'm going. It's best to depend on oneself when in trouble.'

'Not rubbish at all. You must say—I need my diary sooooo much. Pleeeease return it. Be coy with specific words, just as I'm showing you. They will inevitably want to meet you to return it.'

'They're doing that already. I told them to come home. Said I'd give them a treat. Still they haven't come.'

'They won't. Ask them to come to the spot I told you about, they'll turn up. Without any objection. Then, at the appointed hour, accept the diary with lots of smiles. Invite them to meet you again.'

'Lovely. And then?'

'And then trust me. Be prepared when you go.'

'What do you mean?'

'I mean don't keep your hair loose or something. Wrap

the end of your sari round your waist. You must be ready to run.'

Esha went as instructed. A green sari with a red border. The end of her sari wrapped around her waist. Parrot green trees and grass, parrot green sari on Esha. Aritra and his gang were observing from a distance. Three louts were saying something to Esha, waving their arms and displaying mouthfuls of teeth. They were a bit flustered by Esha's presence. She was probably not the kind of feminine personality who made their talents flower. One of them gave her the diary. And Aritra and his companions approached them slowly from the back.

'When will you come again? You must give separate dates to each of us.'

Now Aritra's group pounced with hockey sticks. Esha disappeared in a flash. So many world wars had been fought over women, but how many of them had been written about outside the epics? At eight-thirty that night Esha appeared in Aritra's tiny coop at their joint family residence. Ari seemed to be asleep. Sticking plaster on his chin and forehead, his mother was saying, 'Why does he have to play hockey? Coming home with bruises.' Ari laughed in his head, his eyes shut. The hockey stick was so potent that trying to thrash the enemy had led to a couple of same-side goals. Esha was leaving, thinking he was asleep. But his acting prowess was preventing him from finding out just which Padavali her gratitude belonged to. Esha, you're a more distant isle, near the stars of the night. How can that same you come so close to me now? This was what Aritra Chowdhury could not grasp. Could she manifest herself in the physical world? No, she could not, Aritra decided in a burst of clarity. Which was why this incredible impossibility was about to become possible. She had driven a bulldozer over his life for eighteen years. Esha was no longer the Esha of the Padavali. Just as Neelam was no longer a Raphael painting either. Why had this obvious truth escaped him? Along with the outer Esha, the inner Esha had changed too. Even the Neelam who had been so exuberant and blossoming and stricken and distressed and detached and engrossed in every bone and tissue of her body eighteen years ago was now a cold block of stone. An unmoving glacier. And even Esha could not possibly have remained the long-lashed, intimate, deep, emotional, steadying blue lightning she had once been. He had no idea how she had spent these eighteen years. He had had no way of knowing. He had always been unwanted in Esha's home. It would have made no sense to enquire there. Still he had kept writing, like setting a series of lamps afloat on the Ganga at Har ki Pauri during evening prayers. The lamps drift away on the currents—kasmai devaya? To which god? Did the intended recipient ever receive it? Was the ethereal half-familiar deity seen dimly through the fumes of incense real? Would he descend from his divine proscenium to a place in full view of human eyes? Was it even possible? Or would there be an accident before that. It could happen to Ari, it could happen to Esha. Deep inside himself, he shivered violently. What if something happened to Esha! Did Ari want her to die? Lest his dream be shattered. No, never. Aritra had the courage to look the truth in the eye. Esha was not the same Esha anymore. A different Esha was on her way. A different Neelam, a different Esha, a different Aritra. The geometry had changed. The old history on the pages would be rubbed out with an eraser to make room for a new one. That was best. This was best. Patil was blowing the horn gently. Adjusting the knot of his tie, Aritra slipped his feet into his shoes. Neelam brought a small packet of holy flowers and touched his forehead with them before putting them in the pockets of his trousers. The door had opened. The old routine after a long time: work, conversations with several people while a Dunhill hangs from his lips, telephone calls, lunch at the gymkhana, inspecting the layouts of advertisements, conferring with Vinay Desai over the visuals. What meaningless tasks and waste of time a man could be absorbed in. The very entrails of civilization had been entangled in the impenetrable evilness of demand for worthless commodities.

FIVE

After the seminar on the first day had ended, Mahanam stood in the small balcony adjoining his room in Chandrashekhar's house. The glare of the late afternoon was palpable. There would be light for a long while yet. Shekhar hadn't been to the seminar today. He had other work. His students were conducting a survey of adolescent children from low-income groups. He was probably at a school in old Pune. He hadn't said whether he would ask his students to prepare the report on returning to the university, or whether he could come home directly. Mahanam had made himself a pot of coffee. He had been feeling tired, but the coffee had revived him. He would go out for a walk after Shekhar was back. He couldn't leave the house empty, though Shekhar had given him a duplicate key. The house had been alone all day. It probably wouldn't be right to abandon it again. Only what lay behind these blocks of flats was visible from this balcony. Slices of the road through the gaps. Beyond the road lay fields, but they had vanished behind a dense growth of greenery. Mahanam went back into his room after a while. He was feeling restless. The visit to Priyalkarnagar was not taking place. He had shown up like a ghost at midnight the first day.

This chair could be tilted back as he pleased. Mahanam reclined it a long way and sat down, his hands clasped behind his head. His house in Duff Lane was the Marble Palace by another name. A trace of mildew had appeared on the black and white floor with the floral pattern. The antique mahogany chairs were intricately carved, without offering the slightest possibility of reclining. Marble-topped tables lay in front of them. Mahanam was saying, 'You know what, Ari, I have tried too many things in one life. I pursued literature while studying medicine, then I got involved in symbolic logic and applied mathematics even before I'd finished my literature course, and now I'm obsessed with homeopathy. Nothing else but the *Materia Medica* running through my head. A one-track mind. I cannot possibly teach you Baudelaire now. And frankly speaking, I'm afraid of Esha.'

'What! Whatever for?' Esha almost jumped out of her chair. Mahanam laughed. 'Girls who study poetry often ask such difficult questions that dilettante teachers like me cannot offer answers.'

Aritra's eyes were still questioning. An intelligent young man, he had not believed the explanation. Mahanam had inadvertently blurted out something that lay deep in his mind. Doubt gathered in Aritra's eyes. Couldn't boys who studied poetry ask difficult questions too?

Yagneshwar had brought in luchi, alur-dom and deep-fried hilsa. All of them white. The first two were milky white. The fish had acquired a golden hue because it had been fried.

'I'm something of a gourmet too,' Mahanam was saying, dividing a luchi into four with a fork and a knife. 'Quite primitive in that sense.'

'Are you going to use a knife and fork for the fish too?' asked Esha in wonder.

'Not knife and fork, but just the fork.' Spearing a piece of fish with his fork, Mahanam transferred it into his mouth. 'Why aren't you eating?'

Aritra took a sip of tea. Esha said, 'Both tea and hilsa are off-limits for me, Mahanam-da.'

'Still on milk?'

'Not just on milk, on luchi and alur-dom too. But I'm not used to such a heavy breakfast at this hour of the morning. Makes me uncomfortable,' Esha replied.

'Yagneshwar!'—Mahanam called for him—'Yagneshwar!' He appeared in a dhoti and shirt, a duster slung over his shoulder, a bristly moustache, and grey hair.

'Never cast pearls before swine. Take away your Begumbahar luchi and Mughlai alur-dom at once. These two think gastronomy and academics are mutual enemies. Let them, but I am not allowing your cooking skills to be humiliated.'

Yagneshwar picked up the tray of food while Esha said, 'Begumbahar luchi? Mughlai alur-dom? What are all these, Mahanam-da?'

'You'd have known if you'd tried them,' answered Mahanam, carefully folding the second luchi with his knife and fork. 'If you can have rumali roti, why not

Begumbahar luchi? Invented by Yagneshwar Mal, esquire. Practically transparent. If you'd only tasted the alur-dom you'd have known it isn't your everyday stuff.'

What had Aria and Esha discussed on their way back that day? A smile appeared on Mahanam's lips. Aritra must have said, 'Actually he doesn't know anything. Claims to know French like his mother tongue. Humph!'

'Strange man, you know.'

'More peculiar than strange. Begumbahar luchi! My foot!'

'No but I should have tasted it. I made a mistake.'

'You made nothing of the sort. He's actually a miser. Complete skinflint. Thinks he's very clever. Just flashed the tray before our eyes. Always does that. Yagneshwar cooks just once during the day and passes it off for breakfast, lunch and dinner. This one Yagneshwar is my cook-cum-servant-cum-cleaner-cum-errands-boy . . .'

This conversation was not entirely imaginary. These were the stories that circulated about Mahanam, who had just returned from Oxford. He quite enjoyed them. Apparently he had grown a beard to hide a burn on his chin. From acid. Which he had acquired when trying to kill himself. Had a colleague not snatched the bottle of hydrochloric acid out of his hands he would have been the late Mahanam by now. And the suicide was apparently for the blue-eyed Irene McCutcheon. Mahanam would hear these stories, but never protest. This was how legends were created. His beard, Joggeshwar, Marble Palace and the strange things he said had given birth to long-standing fables on the university campus—he found it all quite amusing.

There was always a kernel of truth in every legend. Her name was Iris, not Irene, she had gifted him a triangular pebble of granite when he was leaving. She said she had picked it up in Salisbury, near Stonehenge. A polished, swollen, triangular stone. Others gave him different sorts of gifts, but Iris gave him a pebble. When he asked her about it, smiling, she said, 'Do you seriously mean you don't recognize it?'

'Seriously.'

'It is my heart that I am giving unto you.'

'And it is made of stone.'

'Oh no. It is as long-lasting and heavy.'

About to burst into trademark laughter, Mahanam became quiet.

'Look, Iris, I look upon you as my sister and friend.'

'Do you people in India kiss your sisters the way you did on Christmas Eve?'

'I beg your pardon. One never knows what one can do under the influence of strong liquor. One doesn't even remember.'

'You needn't beg my pardon, Nam. We are used to being jilted ever since the goddamned war. Men have thousands to choose from.'

Iris gave him a gift of an entire heated heart, as heavy as granite. If there had to be an acid burn on the chin, it should have been on Iris's, not Mahanam's. His students had heard the opposite of what had happened. The truth was that they could not imagine spurning a white woman. And Mahanam hated the familiar tale of going to 'Blighty' and returning as a white man with a white woman in tow as wife. But coming as she did from the land of Annie Besant, Margaret Noble, and Maud Gonne, how could Iris have said so easily, we are used to being jilted? This was some sort of feminine complex. There was no basis to such ideas. Mahanam had always considered women equal in every respect. He knew nothing about having a sister, the sister whom he had invoked to fob Iris off. In his youth there must have been an excess of emotion in the hidden recesses of his mind over family relationships. But he did not know the taste of parents or siblings. Although his knowledge of governesses or friends was more than a hundred per cent.

Mahanam had a broad forehead. If not quite like Ishwarchandra Vidyasagar's, nor hairless, it was expansive. The sharpness of his nose was evident. His chin was small in comparison. Every time he shaved his mirror would scold: divide the canvas into two. If you overload the upper half with so much colour, the balance will be destroyed. That was when Mahanam began to grow a beard. A nice, black, wavy beard, which he had to trim every day to match with his face when he was at Trinity College. When he returned, bearded, his friends couldn't recognize him. Not just his appearance, they claimed his entire personality had changed because of the beard covering his face.

Sambaran would say, 'What is this Oxo-Iranian personality you've created for yourself. I feel like I have to look at you through a telescope. Get rid of the beard.'

Mahanam would reply, 'Why don't you understand that even without the beard I'd be the same person. It's the personality that's changed, though not entirely—that's a misconception on your part. It just seems that way at first, but everything will fall into place later.' And Sandeep said, 'Say what you will, I am a hundred per cent sure there's a mystery behind it. Why else should you object so strongly to shave a mere beard? If it had at least been a moustache—a moustache maketh the man.'

'It's the same with the beard. If you are recognizable by your bushy moustache, you might as well spot me by my beard.'

The mystery surrounding Mahanam had probably begun with his beard. Sandeep's use of the word mystery had led to speculation in different circles. Mahanam had never said, 'I don't care for the way my chin looks, so I grew a beard to conceal it.' His laughter was eloquent. Mahanam was wont to play with an excess of words, which made it difficult to extract personal statements. Moreover, he laughed often, not always with joy or enjoyment. It was a mystery, therefore.

There was indeed a mystery about his origins. With no sign of his parents anywhere, he could easily have been called a bastard. At eighteen his Kasturi Mashi had said, 'Don't even ask. There's no end to what people do and how far they can go. You were born without mishap, and the very next night your mother ran away. Her address turned out to be false. After some time in the hospital I brought you home. I didn't adopt you or give you my name—how could you be Mahanam if you already had a name? For this reason alone I didn't teach you to address me as Ma. One day there would be that dramatic moment when you'd learn I'm not your mother. Followed by a whole lot of melodrama and the torment of sentimentality and indigestion. Your parents are dead, Mahanam, and that is the truth. You'd better not become Karna or someone like that. Don't spend the rest of your life like the hero of a novel in search of his mother. You were born on your own strength, not anyone else's. The world sent you free of preliminary bonds. Such good fortune doesn't come easily. Don't ever let yourself be tied down easily. But whoever it was who gave birth to you, they had good genes, you know.' Kasturi Mashi would laugh.

Mahanam was a precocious adolescent then. Perhaps it was because of this background, but he felt no relationship with anyone else—nor did he feel the urge to forge one. Whatever he got, he grasped with both hands. And distributed generously whatever he had. Still people called him a miser. Iris certainly had. All his friends used to complain. Beneath a torrent of words, eating and drinking, and joining discussions and arguments, he was a tortoise in its shell. Only those who tried to get very close realized that his heart was wrapped in an iron curtain. All arrows were stopped there—offensive arrows as well as arrows of love.

Mahanam often felt as though he were visiting this planet on a holiday. Or on work. Just like he had been to Oxford. Just like he had travelled across different European cities. Only the house in Duff Lane gave him the sense of an anchor. Was it because of his extensive travels? Or because he had no one to call his own? Or because of his nature? Chandrashekhar had laughed it off though. But this emptiness, which he experienced after his Mashi's death, worried the forty-plus Mahanam at times. Even family men who carried the weight of many people, of many problems, were not happy. He had observed the laughable lengths to which people would go to escape from their parents or siblings or wife and children. Was Mahanam really rootless in this world? Should he have had some ties too—if only to experience a distaste for them? Was it not a matter of fortune, then, to secure a double-promotion in the university of life?

SIX

The phone buzzed like a cricket. The afternoon vigil had long ended. All the work was done, as were the meals. Digestion was done too. Listening to ghazals with drowsy eyes was done. Aritra was in his office. Pupu, in college. Like they were every day. Exactly like every day, three months ago. The house had returned to its rhythm. The beat had been missing, but now it was back in place. Such peace. Neelam was cutting fabric for a blouse. Scissors, a measuring tape, and a tailor's chalk lay on the table. The blouse was dark brown. There would be scallops on the back and the arms. The iron was warm and ready. The scallops would not come out well otherwise. The phone was ringing.

'It's me. From Thane. Why the urgent summons?'

'No particular reason, just spend a couple of days with us,' said Neelam warily.

'Where? At your house?'

'As if we have space in our humble abode. It's not like you don't have your own house here.'

'You needn't have continued to live in your humble abode, Bhabi. I've been telling you for years to leave it to "Super Seal". I'll make you a palace. You could have paid at your convenience. You needn't even have paid. It was only to satisfy Chowdhury Sahib's ego that . . .'

'Suppose you built us a palace with your own money, what would we tell the income-tax people if they questioned us?'

'Oh Bhabi! Chowdhury Sahib is the P.R.O. of a huge multinational. He could well own plenty of property. Do you keep track? Leave all these little things to Seal. Now tell me what's going on.'

'Can't I just want to see you and Seema? Ari's recovered from such a serious accident. We need to celebrate.'

'Is Ari Chowdhury inviting me to celebrate his recovery? News of the year!'

'Please come. I was thinking of a short holiday to Mahabaleshwar or Matheran. Or Goa.'

'If it's Matheran you want to visit, come over. And madam, your mood doesn't quite seem to match Matheran or Mahabaleshwar, or Goa! Two of them are in the hills, one by the sea. You seem bewildered.'

'Let my mind wander, I'll do what my heart tells me to.'

'Right now is it me your heart wants?' Intensely.

Neelam said, 'So be it. I can't argue with you.' Neelam sitting behind Bikram, the scooter speeding through the air. You shop for groceries every day Bhabi. Let's shop for happiness today.

'Why the deadline of twentieth March?'

'One of my old girlfriends is visiting after a very long

time. We'll have lots of fun together, all of us.'

'Is the girlfriend alone in her dark room?'

'So it seems. Bring Seema and come over.'

'If I bring Seema how will your solitary reaper find a partner?'

'She will, she will. You needn't worry. Just come and . . .' Neelam was about to say 'save my life', but changed it to the more formal 'rescue me'.

'Let me see if I can.'

'As if you run a huge business empire or something. If you leave the cards with a dummy for a few days will you earn fewer cases of black money?'

'Careful Bhabi, you can't taunt me about black money.'

'All right, all right, your money is white as driven snow. All right? Bye now.'

'No no. Will the universe collapse if you talk a little longer? Your voice is just the same. Like birdsong. Let me hear it a little longer. I feel a tingle.'

Neelam put the phone down. Beads of perspiration had appeared on her brow. Your voice is just the same. Even Bikram had told her how much about her had changed. Only the voice hadn't. The old Neelam did not exist. Nothing left of her. Neither in form, nor in nature. But if that were so, why were Bikram's hands shaking as he answered the phone? Was it out of fear—the fear of doing something in secret? Still? Or was it romance? Bikram's voice, seeing him in her mind's eye, churned the foam in her memory. A powerful, forceful, strong, desirous man, with firm, fleshy lips, extremely garrulous, his song was not music, it was an expression of physical desire.

Lutf uske badan ka kuchh nah puchho
Kya jaaniye, jaan hai keh tan hai

Such indescribable pleasure from his touch, is it of the spirit or is it physical?

How many women lived within one? Like rabbits from a magician's hat, or like white pigeons from a fist, they appeared on different cues. Aritra got one Neelam every morning and evening. The Neelam who responded to Bikram on the phone was a completely different one. Which Neelam was Pupu's mother? Which Neelam had emerged at the possibility of Esha's arrival? And which Neelam was it whom Mahanam had called out to that night? Besides these there was also Neelam Joshi Chowdhury, president of the Bijoya Dashami reception committee. Mandal, Shah, Iyengar or Khadelkar's Neelam Bhabi. Neelam rose suddenly, going up to the mirror. All the furniture in this house was multipurpose, there was no such thing as a separate dressing table. There was a tall mirror in Ari's bedroom. A round one in Pupu's. Cosmetics for daily use were in a drawer in the desk next to the mirror. The rest were stored in Pupu's box bed. The mirror was the only object in this house that Neelam did not clean with care. This tall mirror. A lace cover was draped on it. It was Mahanam who used to say: the splitting image of Jane Morris. I've never seen such resemblance. Jane Morris was Dante Gabriel's friend's wife and, like his own, the model of many of his paintings. Mrs Rossetti died so beautifully in her youth, why couldn't Neelam have done the same? Dying early keeps a woman an object of love, romance and desire forever. She had hoped to die on the operation table. Her blood count was low. Her blood group was a rare one, she had needed several bottles. Two tables packed with empty bottles of blood and saline. Only Pupu's face would float before her eyes in her semi-conscious state. What would happen to Pupu then, would a doll always come between every mother and her death wish? Pupu! Pupe! Why did you come? Whom do you belong to? Are you my sin? And yet you are all the forgiveness for all my sins. Who says there can be no forgiveness. Didn't Aritra like to read the poet who said, 'And yet there is forgiveness. Only forgiveness. It harbours no regrets.' Would the godhead not forgive her if she begged with shame, clasping Pupu to her breast? Humans rued being 'unable to forgive', but god forgave. Forgive them, my father, for they know not what they do. No, no. Neelam was startled. It was humans who forgave. God did not. The youthful allure with which she had played her game had not been taken away by another human, but by him. He sent people with certain priceless assets. Health, beauty, intelligence, talent. And then he went off on a long vacation instead of waiting to be consulted or to control. He would come back one day to tot up the accounts. What have you done with your assets, Neelam Joshi? Would Neelam be able to stand in front of him with her curly hair at whose roots nature was sprinkling grains of talcum powder, with her rose-smooth skin that had been stretched so tight it seemed close to breaking, with her vital statistics of 40–38–48? Would she be able to tell him, look, my lord, this is what I have done with the assets you gave me. No, it would be better to keep herself in the background and thrust Pupu forward. Just as Yashodhara had thrust Rahul. The fiery girl was dark, wide-eyed, snub-nosed, curious but resolute. Pushing her forward, Neelam would say, this is what I have created. Check for yourself whether what you had given me has multiplied manifold or not. If Pupu stood there with her Sartre and Yeats, her collection of the Upanishads, Gora and Religion of Man, holding a T-square, would the godhead not say, but Neelam, the capital I invested in you has not grown with interest, you are offering me the enhancement of someone else's assets. Everyone in the world said Pup had not inherited anything from either of her parents. Not her father's attractive restlessness, nor her mother's beauty, which lit up the world, nothing. She was different. All Neelam knew fully was the agony of bearing her in her womb for nine months, the pain of giving birth to her.

Opening the drawer, Neelam took out a comb and a brush. She was combing her hair. Untangling the knots, she was brushing it now. The more she brushed, the more it swelled, exactly like a river at high tide. It billowed, like the goddess Kali's locks. Her oily skin as taut as the surface of an inflated balloon. No powder, no make-up stayed, everything fell off. With great care, Neelam was putting on a deep layer of lipstick on the thick but curved lips on her pink, oily face. So scarlet that the teeth behind them had lost the honour of their whiteness. Eyeliner, mascara, golden grey eye-shadow. Taking off her housecoat, Neelam put on the bright red sari which Bikram had bought her from Bangladesh for 1526 Taka ten years ago. Bikram would say, it's a murderous colour,

Bhabi, everything will turn red. Silver keys tucked in at her waist, thin golden bangles covering her arms, a necklace of discs around her neck, a choker at her throat, ear rings with peacock motifs. Much of Aritra Chowdhury's bank balance was now on Neelam's arms and around her neck. Neelam cleaned the mirror carefully with a moist sheet torn out of a newspaper. But! Who was this! Goddesses did not have human dimensions. Their idols were much larger than people. Durga, Lakshmi, Jagatdhatri. Who could claim that these were the only criteria of beauty! Don't be upset, Neelam Joshi Chowdhury. Never accept someone else's judgement. Check for yourself. You can still conquer the world if you want to. You can conquer Aritra, you can conquer Mahanam, Bikram is already in your grasp.

Even after much thought Neelam could not decide which of these victories was imminent and which, essential. Her afternoon passed in a trance, sunk in a daydream. Now she had a mysterious smile on her face at the sight of the battle between Shumbha and Nishumbha, the next moment she looked down at Achilles's valour, at Hector's bravery, from the ramparts of the palace of Troy and told herself, all this is for me. At other times she walked in all her glory between the amassed armies of the Kurus and the Pandavas, unable to decide which of them was Aritra and which, Mahanam. All she could hear were cries of triumph from a distance. Or the weeping of many, many men who wanted her. Both the roars and the sobs wove her daydream, but her mind rejected them. She just could not extract her preferred response from the imagination of the men, she just could not. Thwarted, she lay down in exhaustion, wondering whether to finally welcome Cleopatra's tiny poisonous wasp.

Returning home at twilight, Aritra found her asleep in this garb. The front door was unlocked but closed. It opened when he pushed it lightly. Ari stood inside for a while in surprise. Was Neelam busy somewhere at the back of the house with the front door unlocked? No matter how quickly she returned, it wasn't safe. Someone else could have entered instead of Ari. Shambhaji patrolled the gate after dark. His working hours would start shortly. The gate was unguarded now. After a short wait Ari locked the door. Taking off his shoes slowly, he entered the bedroom, his feet aching and long-unaccustomed to being used. And was overcome with fear as soon as he did. Neelam was lying on the bed, all dressed up. Her hair spread over the pillow. Wearing a silk sari, sindoor smeared on her forehead as though a married woman had dressed up to die. Just before climbing on the pyre. Death by choice. Was this what Neelam had in mind? Aritra couldn't produce a sound. He lifted the receiver to phone the doctor. Put it down again. Then, gathering all the courage at his disposal, he put his hand on Neelam's forehead. Living, warm, sweet, compassionate, without the distance or detachment of death. 'Neelam! Neelam!'

Neelam sat up with a start, rubbing her eyes. When she saw Aritra she said, 'What's wrong? Why are you looking like that?'

Aritra said, 'I should be the one asking you. What's the matter? Why are you in bed like this?'

With bewildered, overwhelmed eyes Neelam observed her own sari, and bangles, turning her hand over to look at the mascara smudged on the back, as though she had dressed up in a dream. She said, 'I had a happy dream, Ari, we were having a Hindu marriage, in front of a fire, with the floor adorned for the seven rounds, you dressed like a groom. In wedding garb, with an embroidered shawl, chandan marks on your brow.'

Their wedding had only involved signing a register and some documents. It was a matter of lifelong regret for the imagination-prone Neelam, who loved ceremony, loved ornaments.

So Aritra said, his voice soft with compassion, 'You can't even imagine how beautiful you're looking, Neelam. Just like a bride, really. Give me a cup of tea now.'

Neelam remained seated the same way, with freshly-awakened eyes, with the aura of dressing up still around her. Her profile was reflected in the mirror. The figure of a dancing deity from Khajuraho. Judging from the bronze figures of danseuses, only in the time of Mahenjodaro was slimness in the body of a woman valued in India. Since then all women had been depicted as heavy hipped and ample breasted. The ideal of the beautiful woman in this country involved plumpness. Neelam forgot everything as she watched herself in the mirror. All her sadness, all her fear, all her guilt from all these years. The twilight streamed in through the west window, sweeping everything away. Then she suddenly saw her own reflection in Ari's glasses. He could no longer hear the call of this hour! The stars were obscured by clouds, Ari's glasses had changed, so farewell was very easy. The defeat of a lifetime. Aritra Chowdhury had forgotten to hear the call. All this dressing up was an illusion, an act of pity. Aritra was leaving the twilight-filled room, a cigarette dangling from his lips.

'Neelam, I want tea, bring some tea, a potful, I'm very thirsty, very.'

Aritra hurried Neelam for the liquid he wanted to pour into his parched throat. Neelam realized that the Greek army was returning, accepting Helen's decision to enter the castle of Troy of her own free will. Agamemnon was going back, Ulysses was going back, Menelaus was going back. They would take Elphinstone Road, cross Holkar Bridge, go past Deccan College and then onto Ahmadnagar Road, heading for Ahmadnagar or Lohagaon.

SEVEN

A complete break for quite some time now from the bonds of books, of listening and cogitating and meditating. Audio-visual experiences outside of daily habit for some time now. As the train plunged into the silence of the night, Esha breathed a sigh of relief, switched off the light above her eyes and lay down in her bunk. A light sheet covered her waist downward. The wind blew in through the open window near her feet. The soles of her feet tingled with the chill. A thrill spread through her. The tingling rose from her skin along the edges of her thin sari to her garments and then across the rest of her body. Even into her blood. Such a pleasure. Ah!

The first afternoon had not proved very difficult. She had turned drowsy, looking out the window through her sunglasses. She had managed to lean back and doze for some time, her face covered by a literary magazine. As evening approached, as the lights were lit, a buzz began in the train. The crunching of peanuts, biscuits, crisps. A child had been playing, he had come up to Esha too. Now suddenly he was screaming, 'Make it whole again.' His young mother had taken a lick of his lollypop, unable to control herself. That was it. His lozenge was damaged. It had to be made whole again. His abashed mother was offering him another one, red, green, blue, each a different colour. But he wouldn't be distracted. He had to have the discoloured yellow lollypop he had been licking. But made whole again. Unable to perform a miracle, the pleas of his disturbed parents turned into annoyed rebuke. His father was shouting in a muted voice. Different groups of people were chatting, their voices merging with the sound of the train, one man's deep voice rising above the others from time to time. 'They used to have chilled water on the Geetanjali earlier.'

Esha sat, lost in the hum of conversations all around her, wrapping her yawning evening languor like a shawl around herself. Her magazine was open in her lap, but the light was so dim that it hurt her eyes to read—all she could do was see the pictures. The lady opposite her asked in Hindi, 'Where are you going?'

'Kalyan.'

'Only up to Kalyan?'

Esha didn't feel like prolonging the conversation. Her travelling companion was quite sociable. Someone or the other was there to meet her at every junction, carrying a tiffin box of either snacks or a meal. She had tried the sandesh Esha had offered her in the afternoon. Now she wanted to share her puri, subzi and pickles with Esha, but because Esha couldn't stomach this sort of food, she turned the lady down courteously and ate the white roti and alu-chochhori that Piku had packed for her in polythene. Piku was unparalleled in these matters. It was difficult to tell whether she was a friend or a mother. For the second day too she had packed fine flattened rice, sweets, and wedges of lime with the seeds removed. Esha glanced sideways at her fellow passengers all evening. Who knew when they would sleep? Maybe they chatted till midnight or watched TV, some of them might even be used to having their dinner after midnight. Eventually, the gentleman in the middle rose to his feet and the man next to him went to the bathroom. Esha rose, stretching herself delicately. Night-long comfort, finally. There could be no one as wise and compassionate as the inventor of sleep. Lying on her bunk, Esha could see the sky with countless stars over open fields, beneath it tiny boxes filled with human drops. The stars were so bright, but they did not wander off, circling and eventually dying in their prescribed orbits, but the droplets of people moved about with irresistible life-force. According to their own wishes. I am one of them. I shall never be still. I shall keep moving and die this way. Is death like the sky? Monochrome, grim? But the application of free will that brings me comfort is not predestined, is it? The world's movement on an orbit is not visible with the naked eye either.

The train raced across the earth like a heated shell. The windows were tightly shut. First only the glass panes had been closed. Now the wooden slats too. A hot wind blew outside. In the darkness of the carriage a compartment full of people panted like dogs with their tongues hanging out.

The young Agarwal boy was off to his uncle's house in Bombay after his school examinations. He had put a wet handkerchief on his face. Now he peeped at Esha, smiling. You could do this too, it'll bring you some relief. She had no objection to learning from people, older or younger. Taking a tiny towel out of her bag, she soaked it in cold water and covered her own face, too. See how I can go one better than my teacher. If yours is a hanky, mine's a towel, it won't dry quickly.

The young man consumed nothing but cold drinks. Esha had bought a vegetarian meal wrapped in aluminium foil. She simply could not eat it. The pulau, daal, potatoes and pickles had all been mashed up together. It would have been best to have been on a diet of fruits and cold drinks like the young man. She had her own food with her too. Piku had said, 'Fine Patna flattened rice, soak it in water and eat with lime juice and sugar. It will cool you.' She had told her, and she had told her again. But Esha wasn't up to such effort in a moving train just to eat. Now, as she transferred the hot mass served on the train from one hand to the other and back, feeling like a fool, she realized that Piku had more experience and practical sense. She should have relied on them. When the two of them had considered building a house in the suburbs, Piku had said with a smile, 'I'll manage your home, you manage my world. But what if you marry?'

Esha had said without a smile, 'Once is enough. But you might marry too.'

Piku was worse than she was, saying seriously, 'Once is enough.'

Both of them had laughed. Putting her arms around Esha, Piku had said,

'Tumi niye chalo amaake lokottore. Tomake bondhu aami lokayete bandhi.'

['Take me away from people, let me bind you amidst them.']

At Nagpur Agarwal bought large oranges, cheap. Finally abandoning his silence, he said, 'The oranges are delicious, taste one, Jiji.' He made Esha buy a dozen. They sat munching on their oranges as the train moved ahead. These Nagpur oranges were far superior to the ones from Darjeeling. And yet Calcutta considered Nagpur oranges inferior. It felt that people from Nagpur kept the best for themselves and sent the poor quality oranges to other places. In West Bengal we do just the opposite. Prawns and honey from the Sunderbans, superior rice from Bardhaman, the best tea from Darjeeling are all exported for foreign exchange. We keep the worst, often inedible, things for ourselves. No one can match us in self-humiliation.

No sooner had they crossed Warba than black, cultivated land became visible on both sides. A balm for the eyes. The Sahayadri had arranged large black rocks on dry riverbeds. Esha gazed in wonder at what looked exactly like a group of small and big elephants emerging from the water after their frolic. How whimsical nature was. It had presented a Jataka tale through wayside sculptures. In the Chaddanta Jataka, Bodhisattva had been born as an elephant with six tusks. There he was, the glorious king of the elephants. But Piku wasn't here. Esha felt no pleasure unless she could share her joy and wonder. Still she kept looking at the scene through the window as long as she could. Subrata Agarwal had realized there was something special out there, but he was not sitting by the window. He had the furthest seat from the window on the bench opposite Esha, he couldn't see anything despite craning his neck. The riverbed was quite low. Eventually he couldn't contain himself any longer and said, 'Something unusual, Jiji?' Esha smiled. 'Nothing unusual, just rocks.'

'That's all?'

'That's all.' How was she to recount the story of the elephant in the Chaddanta Jataka, and its sculptural depiction through the boulders of the Sahayadri, to young Agarwal across the length of the compartment?

The train was passing through one tunnel after another. Each time it entered the darkness, Esha welcomed it as she thought of the threatening moment when she would meet Ari. And when the train emerged into the light, the fear dissipated. She had been through a lot in life. Why should she be afraid? Someone seemed to be saying to the rhythm of the train, *abhi bhava, abhi bhava*. At once Esha became completely calm. Then she wondered why she had wired Aritra. She could have taken a bus from Jalgaon. Or she could have asked a travel agent to make arrangements. Their itineraries involved visiting a different place every day. This form of travel was never satisfying, which was why Esha avoided travel agents despite the assurance they offered. Why did she have to make Aritra her agent? In one letter after another Ari had written, 'Friendship is very valuable, Esha. Friendship is the last word. Can't we be friends? Just friends. Time is infinite, and the world is enormous, life is so short in comparison. The harshness of refusing friendship does not suit you.'

The train was running late. What would she do if there was no one there when she arrived late at night? She could pay extra money to spend a day or two at the Bengal Lodge and sort things out after that. No, the train would reach Victoria Terminus even later at night. Never mind, we'll see what happens. As the train swayed from side to side, Esha went to the toilet in preparation of getting off. Subrata Agarwal looked up at her and smiled. Mrs Jain shifted her huge body to make room. Manmad, Nashik Road, Igatpuri . . .

The long-expected train was finally reaching Kalyan. The clanking of the wheels was slowing down, getting heavier. Esha's feet stuck to the floor of the compartment. Like walking in a dream, she was moving forward but not advancing. Suddenly Subrata appeared from the back and took her light suitcase. Esha only had her bag on her shoulder. She stood still in the frame of the carriage door for some time. The platform was busy. The Geetanjali Express had arrived late, the entire platform was active, noisy, on the move. Where was Aritra? How would she recognize him if he had changed a lot? A gap of eighteen years. Life had changed, people's appearances had changed, the environment had changed, on what basis had she taken this plunge into the unknown? The platform was not particularly long. Esha could not spot a familiar face or familiar gesture amongst all these strangers. She kept walking with slow footsteps, kept walking, holding a fibre suitcase, a bag slung over her shoulder, Esha kept walking.

Aritra had seen her from a distance, though, seen her from afar. From the time that Esha was a bright yellow spot near the furthest star, at the door of her carriage. Aritra looked at her in wonder, standing still. Esha was coming, but eighteen years had not elapsed. She was standing at the same spot where she had said goodbye. The same corner in the right wing of the supper floor of the Coffee Shop. It was from that exact spot that Esha was approaching him. A pensive mass of hair on her shoulder. Not quite visible, a thin curtain of moist, bluish cloud, the sun shining through it. The rhythm of her movement shook the universe of Aritra's attention to the core.

You come from a new age, from the heart of womanliness, awakening from your charmed sleep
Silencing the armies of time with a signal from your divine mouth
You come with the terrifying inevitability of a nuclear storm
Like a tumultuous rebellion you come like the contagion of a million viruses in blood cells

This was what an engrossed, hypnotized Aritra was reciting softly when Esha reached him where he stood, still and unmoving. Railway workers, porters and passengers walked past the eulogist, none of them paying him any attention. Aritra didn't pay them any either. Just as a water-laden cloud showers firebolts from time to time, lightning began to flash in Esha's heart as she listened to the mesmerized song of praise. She wanted to scream,

'You're lying. Not I, it was you, you who used to come this way, like an unwelcome virus, unwanted but irresistible. Contagious. Making my blood rise in extreme, intoxicated rebellion. Your dishevelled hair raising a thousand hoods like the offspring of a king cobra, your forehead invisible, your nose like a sharpened sickle, your eyes like slits. Drunk, verdant, vernal, mutinous. A constant flow of words like smoke from a Charminar, a cyclonic storm, the torrent of a waterfall in the mountains, streaking like a bus on a highway, rumbling, sometimes a light drizzle, tinkling autumn flowers, unceasing, accurate, and, again, a hundred times irresistible.'

Travelling along Upper Circular Road, the car had turned left at Vivekananda Street and then into Cornwallis Street. In her absent-mindedness she hadn't noticed, but to their left were Dasgupta, International and Chakraborty Chatterjee, rows of bookshops, the pavement, students with tired faces thronging the railings, the inevitable professor with a portfolio bag and dark glasses, researchers—how could you still not recognize the neighbourhood of College Street? It had been exactly five years. Back home after five years. And yet those five years were an entire age. Five years of a strict vow to forget so many things. Not from very far away, however, only from the treasury of the world, West Asia. Money and leave to go home every year were always available. She had spent it visiting whichever of the Gulf countries she could, and leapfrogging through India, Burma, Singapore, Hong Kong and Japan. She hadn't even considered returning home. Those days what Esha thought was what Esha did, that was how it was. Her husband was exactly seventeen years, three months and five and a half days older than her.

She said to the chauffeur Gobindolal, 'Can you stop for a minute, Gobindo-da, I want to get off for a bit.'

It was difficult to park on the road, so the car turned into Colootola Street. Esha returned to the world of books. She was enveloped in the sharp odour of old volumes, the petrichor of new editions. Fat guidebooks for students at every kiosk, paper, maps, flowers, birds, vehicles, superheroes.

'What do you need, Didi, which book?'

'Just tell us what you want.'

An overly enthusiastic young man offered her a stool, saying, 'All the guidebooks for the English fifth paper are out, Didi. Complete in one volume.'

Heaven knew why they had considered Esha a student or a teacher in search of guidebooks for the English fifth paper. She still gave off a scent of luxury, of a foreign country. Students or teachers didn't exude such fragrances. The glow of her skin was the kind that could be seen only on those who had been abroad recently. Those who spent all their hours from morning till night in air-conditioned rooms, who had not encountered contaminated drinking water, who had long become accustomed to unadulterated food and cosmetics.

Dissuading the young man, she entered Bankim Chatterjee Street. She didn't know why. People never went to the Coffee House by themselves. Nor was this a suitable road to walk around on. She could pass the University Institute, go around the Mahabodhi Society, and enter

Colootola Street through the other end of College Square. At least she would circle College Square like a temple. It was a part of her alma mater, after all. Like a piece of iron drawn to a magnet, her eyes suddenly flew towards the showcase of her once-favourite bookshop. A slim book, of double-demy size. The indecipherable face of a woman on the cover, a cross between Picasso and Jamini Roy. The book was titled 'For Presha'. Esha entered the shop like a robot, buying the book for eleven and a half rupees. It was quite expensive, considering it was barely thirty-two pages. The quality of the paper was excellent. The poems were accompanied by indistinct images drawn with a mixture of thin and thick strokes.

Esha returned to the car with the book. Quickly. For some reason she felt it was unsafe to wander around here. It was a jungle. Ancient, violent, infested with wild animals. Bloodthirsty, feral carnivores. So the Preshas were still alive? Could they be alive? But where would she go? Was it yet possible anywhere in the world for a woman to sit by herself in undisturbed solitude? She had to ponder. Finally she told Gobindo, 'Can you take me to Victoria for a bit?'

In the rear-view mirror she saw his furrowed brow.

'Victoria? Alone, Boudi?'

'You could stay nearby. I really want to.'

'Wouldn't it be better to go with Dada?'

'The evening will have ended by then Gobindo. Please take me.'

Gobindo must have concluded that his employer had married an eccentric woman. But he turned out to have been right. Esha could not spend any time at all at Victoria

Memorial. For one thing, it was incredibly crowded and dirty. For another, the inquisitiveness. Practically every single man surveyed the woman with the book as he passed. Many of them made comments. Some of them based on deep research into her relationship with Gobindo. She couldn't remain there. Gobindo drove her home grimly.

Having announced her arrival, Esha turned her back to a pair of frowns, entered her room and shut the door. A deep veranda ran along its side. She drew a chair to it and sat down. The tenth floor of a multistorey building. It seemed to be leaning against the sky. It was nearly six, but there was still daylight. By that light she read the name of the poet. Trilokesh Gaurav. She was right. This Presha was the same Presha. A sharp thrust of the sword on the dedication page—for Presha, 'For Presha, For Presha.' Suddenly Esha felt as though the pointed edge of the sword had penetrated her heart and buried itself to the hilt. Only the glittering handle was visible. Blood was gushing out. In spurts. Had there been so much blood in Esha's body, then? Had there been such an ache in her heart? Was it still there? Could it still be there? Could these drops of undigested emotion infiltrate the bloodstream like cholesterol? She lay with her face buried in the pillow for a long time, raising her head slowly from the river of blood. Closing her hand around the handle of the sword, she tried with all her strength to pull it out, like uprooting a gigantic, demonic thorn, and to fling it away as far as possible in exhaustion. Far away. The letters floated like dust smotes in the fading light:

'You come from another age, awakening from magic sleep in the heart of a woman's consciousness . . .' The late afternoon light had turned drowsy. There seemed to be a layer of bright crystal around Esha, both separating her from and uniting her with the world. She could see everything, but it all seemed like a reflection in the water. Tossing in a pebble could make it all disappear in an instant. She felt as though she was dressed in an astronaut's vacuum suit. Weightless. Floating. The menacing sky was filled with millions of stars. The ecliptic. Unwanted, dangerous ultraviolet rays from the sun were constantly striking and exploding. But still, what was this madness in the blood? Why this drowsiness when the environment was so threatening, so dangerous?

Space rocket	empty pocket
Closed orbit	fully fit
High centre	show the monitor
It's your move	idiot-proof
Words that clash	dot dash dash
Dash dot dot	words that clot
Soft landing	tra la la ling
Is this Venus	or Haiti
Or Dallas	strange psyche

Esha closed the book in extreme exhaustion. This idiom was familiar to her, this Morse Code. Esha knew this meaningful frivolousness, she was conversant with the electric signals beneath the drollery. All this eloquence made her nauseous now. With its love from the past.

With a sigh Esha looked at Aritra. The uncontrollable hair, once like the mane of a lion, was disciplined now.

It had taken on the colour of faded rust that precedes grey hair. The bright, emotional eyes were hidden behind glasses. The framework of the lean cheeks had swollen. Aritra no longer seemed as tall, he had shrunk. Smiling, Esha said, 'Whom am I looking at? The poet Trilokesh Gaurav, or the executive Aritra Chowdhury?'

Aritra could not speak. He couldn't say out loud what he was saying in his head. All he could say softly was, 'Poets never die entirely. So you've finally come, Esha? To me?'

Raising her eyes, Esha said, 'I have. But not just to you. How is Neelam? How old is your daughter?' Esha observed in surprise how easily she could utter Neelam's name now. And as soon as she could a load was lifted off her, and Esha walked faster. She said, 'I made you come all this way. But why are you limping?'

Aritra said, 'I had an accident. Almost recovered now. It's nothing.' He didn't say that he had been close to death, who knew whether it would make any difference to Esha if the life that belonged to Neelam was lost.

Esha slowed down, not asking any more questions. Aritra said, 'We've missed the earlier train. Geetanjali was very late today. We have to take the last train. It'll reach at midnight. Wait here while I go get the tickets.'

It was very crowded. Siddheshwar Express was overflowing. This was the last train to Kohlapur today. Having found Esha a place to sit, Aritra stood wedged in near the door. The train was speeding along, Esha could hear Aritra chatting with a fellow passenger. 'Oh no. She is not my wife. But a great friend. I could easily lay down my life for her . . . Yes . . . that's right. We are meeting after eighteen years. Can you imagine?' The Maharashtrian man looked at Esha out of the corner of his eyes. Was Aritra drunk, wondered Esha.

The train climbed the hills slowly in the darkness. The air cooled, became purer. A necklace of lights ran alongside.

Patil took the suitcase from Aritra, his eyes questioning. Aritra said, 'Geetanjali was incredibly late. And now it's very late at night, you'd better go home.' Patil was very keen on going home. But he wasn't sure if it was all right to abandon his boss. 'Come, I'll drop you home,' said Aritra.

Aritra's car moved along Pune's cold blue night. He was driving after a long time. He felt as though it was not a car that he was steering but a boat. Let this journey never end. What a wonderfully magical, tremulous, fragrant night! Not earthly. Nor heavenly. This was somewhere in between. Where the demigods lived—the kinnars, or yakshas, or gandharvas. Mingling with the wind, they were wandering about on this mysterious midnight. They might well be visible suddenly in the headlights of the car. The poetry he had lost many years ago seemed to be enveloping him now, entrancing him. Its majestic glory was infinite. Even now, even now. Even in the middle of this tired night.

Esha thought about the number of times they had sat next to each other like this in trams and buses and taxis, tuning the rhythms of their bodies to the rhythm of the moving vehicle. Knots that did not bind. The sea at low tide with a ruinous breeze, a random wind. A salty tang on the skin. The salt from the water on the brow, the cheeks, between the fingers, the elation of speed in both hands. Beyond the crest and trough of the breakers, the deep, transparent blue water, the covert currents pulling her from the shore into the depths, the cape like Kali's protruding, pointed tongue, an undiscovered virgin forest on a deserted island. An eruption from the crater of one live volcano to another.

Tales of such daredevilry reached the Khan family at the appointed time. The matriarch fainted with loathing. Rebuke, confinement. Grapes were wrapped in cotton wool, possibly for protection. But no one considered the fact that cocooning people this way was likely to lower their immunity. Even if the windows were closed, the storm always raged when it had to. Lifting the slats, it had roared its way into the ears. A storm of these dimensions usually dislodged the boulders lying along the path of routine and left only after changing the direction of life.

Her friends were saying, 'Be careful, Esha. You're not Aritra Chowdhury's only goddess. There were others earlier, there will be more later. From undergraduate to postgraduate, from postgraduate to research scholar, the history of Aritra Chowdhury aka. Trilokesh Gaurav has remained unchanged.'

Aritra was striding along, his hair flying in the wind, the corners of his eyes had narrowed, he was saying, 'What lovely curls this Neelam girl has. What a wondrous curve to her lips. I've never seen anything like this. Have you, Esha?'

Esha was saying, 'When are you marrying me, Ari?'

'Suddenly? Out of the blue?'

'You weren't expecting this, were you?'

'The things you say, Esha! Don't you know you are my heart?'

'I know, Ari. I am your lungs, digestive system, spleen, liver, and perhaps your intestines, small and large, at the moment.'

'What a horrible thing to say, Esha. Haven't you seen how I live? Haven't you known it for the past four years? Uncles and their families everywhere, I have to pass my days in the room beneath the stairs, haven't you seen all this? I'll die if I have to get a job.'

'Very well, continue with your writing. I'll work till you're established.'

'You'll work? Nine to five? White sari? Black bag? Small umbrella?' Gaurav the poet gazed in fear at his goddess.

Esha said, 'What kind of poet are you? You are afraid of the truth, you hate reality. You're an escapist. Poetry cannot come from escape.'

'I'm not an escapist Esha. I'm a poet with a mission. The age we live in does not have the power to reject me. Poetry is a sort of psychiatry. To penetrate the mind of the age, to mesmerize it with the power of words, to transport all its guilt and its suffering for piety from an unconscious state to a conscious one—the poet has many responsibilities. It is impossible to dress smartly and go to office in such cases.'

'Tell the truth, Aritra. Why are you lying? The truth is that your objective has changed.'

'Are you talking of Neelam Joshi? Oh Esha, I can never make you understand that you are my sacred leaf, moist with the first morning dew on a holy copper plate. Totally unpolluted.' The poet's voice was soaked in passion. 'Entangled in your hair is the moss from a thousand secret oceans that will never see the sun, like the heart of a pearl-bearing shell you are untouched by the sun, unsullied by sin. While Neelam is the fragrant lime in the child widow's garden. The piety of her body and heart is the stuff of her passion.'

'And so you sullied me?' Her eyes blazed fire. Trilokesh's eyes were clouded, his voice like thunder. 'You have not been sullied, Esha, I did not touch you, my poetry did, I did not want you consciously, my poetry did. And nothing can be purer than poetry.'

'How many women do you need for poetry, Ari?' Scraping her chair back, Esha rose. Like a flash of lightning she passed through the corridor, like a taan from a raga she leapt up the stairs in a swift rhythm. She was gone. Gone forever.

That was Esha's first coronary thrombosis. A private explosion through a silent scream emerging from a cave. Flames, raging flames. Each of her nerves was a cauldron of fire. Burning, everything was burning.

Her brother advertised in the papers. She chose the groom herself from the responses. Seventeen years, three months and five and a half days older than her, down to the day. Full of gravitas. Responsible. Stable.

Aritra said, 'So you did see the book.'

Esha said, 'Book? Not books?'

'The first. And the last.'

'Then your prediction didn't come true? The age did not accept you after all, Aritra? And you did take up a job? Nine to five. Ration bags, dusting the cobwebs, baby-food?'

Looking into the distance miserably, Aritra said, 'Poets

never die entirely, Esha. They merely go underground, like seeds in winter. Why did you have to go away, Esha? At once? Why were you in such a hurry? If you hadn't, you'd have realized that poets are human too. And all humans make mistakes. The book had possessed me, Esha. I looked for you like a madman to give it to you. And you not only went away, you went all the way to Bahrain.'

There was no sindoor in Esha's hair now. To skirt the issue of Bahrain, Aritra said quickly, 'Still, you did get the book. Weren't you pleased? Esha-Presha. The book was for you.'

In her head Esha said, 'Oh Aritra, don't you know? That book was never meant for me. It was I who was meant for it. The giant bacteria had fed on all the blood in my corridors and windows, my oxygen passages, the entire slippery discharge from my pituitary, my thyroid, my adrenal, the movement of the mysterious entity named intelligence in every cell of my brain, each of the reflexes in my nerves. I ripped up its pages and flung the pieces away. I twisted the covers out of shape and tore into them with my teeth. With a knife I sliced the colourful Picasso face so that the fiery syntax of the words were wiped out completely and forever.'

Insects of the night buzzed in the green light on the avenues. Priyalkarnagar was sunk in slumber. Many significant events take place at night, while the world sleeps. Serious illnesses, deaths, births, lovemaking, all of these take place. Hidden away from the sleeping people, an important event was taking place in Aritra Chowdhury's life. Block B. Shambhaji had swung open the illuminated gate. The curtains on Pupu's window parted at the sound. The sound of a door being opened. The frosted bulb in the ceiling of the portico was circular, its light pouring a stream of milk over Pupu's well-formed head. There was a halo of light around her head, like a saint's.

'Baba! How late you are! Ma's been crying in anxiety!'

A cool, pleasant voice. A lot like an adolescent boy's. Esha was the first one to get out of the car and step forward. Aritra was taking his boots off. Taking Pupu's hand, Esha said, 'Your father had to go to a lot of trouble on my account. If I'd known it was so far away I'd never have made such a demand. I'd have gone on to VT, stayed the night, and taken the Deccan Queen.'

Pupu said, 'Come inside, Mashi. Ma has become very shaky ever since Baba's accident. In any case she's very superstitious. She was crying and calling your name, Esha, Esha.'

Neelam wasn't actually crying anymore. But her face was grey. She sat on the sofa like a corpse. Esha remained where she was. She seemed unable to take another step unless Neelam rose and called out to her. It was agonizing to appear in her vicinity. Neelam sat invincible within a circle of fire. Both their faces were scalded by the heat.

The sight of Aritra standing behind Esha with her suitcase forced Neelam to stand up with great effort. Looking at Aritra, her face ashen, she said, 'I thought you had had another accident.'

'Rubbish,' said Ari. 'An accident is just that, an accident. It occurs only once in a lifetime. Geetanjali was incredibly late. Thankfully we could take the Siddheshwar. Else I doubt whether we'd have been able to return tonight.'

'Something terrible would have happened to Ma in that case Baba,' said Pupu.

Esha said, 'Come here, Neelam, how are you?' Suddenly she reached out and hugged Neelam. How fragrant Neelam's curly hair was. The scent of trembling surrender. A silken warmth, just like a bird, fluttered in Esha's breast. Intimate, sweet. They deposited their sorrows, fears and doubts with each other. And then, uttering a silent vow in unison, they turned to look at Aritra.

EIGHT

Esha had acquired a girlish animation. She woke up early, before everyone else, changing her clothes quietly, wondering for a minute or two whether it would be right to go out leaving the front door unlocked. Then she remembered Shambhaji. Since he was on the night shift, he was bound to be there till eight at least. Closing the door gingerly behind her, she had a chat with the guard at the main gate, requesting him to keep an eye on the door.

An open road, lined with trees, its smooth surface free of dust. Someone had said that his favourite hobby was walking. He was right. Walking was worthy of becoming a passion. You're walking, the morning breeze leaving fleeting touches on you, ever so slightly wintry, and the inevitable scents of unfamiliar plants and trees, birds, the sky mingled with the breeze. You'll try to grasp it but you cannot, it will startle you, raise questions in your mind, and run away. Scattered thoughts will appear in your head as accompaniments to this breeze and these leisurely footsteps. Hill Cart Road, with boulders on the verge. The mountain ranges in the distance, visible through gaps in the pines and firs. Mall Road in Mussoorie, the hill rising on one side, and hotels, houses and deodar trees on the other. Why had she thought of Thomas Hardy's Tess while walking along Hill Cart Road? The same thoughts came back to her now. There were two kinds of planets—sick and healthy. Which one was ours? Sick. The young Tess was telling her brother all this. Esha did not know why all this came to mind. Along with Mussoorie, she was also reminded of Girindrasekhar Bose's *Purana-Pravesh* with its historical explanation of the myth of Bhagiratha's creation of the Ganga. What if a complete picture of ancient India could be drawn by explaining mythology through history? Oh, did Bajirao's horse canter down these roads? Perhaps these were just mountain trails at the time, not flat roads like today.

No sooner had she turned a corner than a mass of light pounced on her. Bathe me in this cascade of light, the poet had written. This was the eastern side. No trees, a wide avenue. Shops on both sides, the corrugated iron door of one of them being rolled up with a clatter. It was an enormous shop—half of Neelam's groceries must come from this one. A bus passed at an unbelievable speed. Esha entered the shop, then strolled back.

They had all gathered in the living room. As soon as Esha entered Pupu said, 'There's Mashi.'

Anxiety all over his face, Aritra said, 'How can you go out in an unknown city without telling anyone? What if you'd lost your way? Or got into trouble?'

'Don't you ever feel tired, Esha?' asked Neelam. 'You

arrived late last night after such a long journey in the heat. And you were off again at the crack of dawn.'

Setting the box of ice cream down on the table, Esha smiled. 'I didn't fly on a jet plane, so no question of jet lag. The fatigue of the journey wore off during the long cool drive last night, believe me. The little sleep I had was very deep. And Neelam, every new place becomes old in three days. That's why you have to get a taste of it the very first day.'

'Becomes old in three days?' exclaimed Neelam. 'Oh god!'

'Yes, as soon as it becomes familiar the romance of the unknown disappears.'

The clouds had lifted from Aritra's expression. He said a little too loudly, 'You've missed the morning tea, Esha, make her some tea with your Gujarati masala, Neelam. Give us some too. And give us a tableful of breakfast. If you're feeling so very well, Esha, I'll send my car back once I get to work. Neelam can show you some of Pune. While it's still new.'

'Yes Mashi, while it's still new,' said Pupu.

In the car Aritra turned the stereo on.

Ai mere zahra zavi, tujhe malum nahi
Tu abhi tak hai haseen aur main jawan . . .

Flame-coloured summer petals were being shed from Esha's head and shoulders on the pavements of Red Road. Picking some of them and finding her way through the rest, Esha walked along a pensive path of colours.

Oh my beloved, you do not know, you do not know that you are still as beautiful and I, still a young man. There was an incantatory dance that everyone performed after a small drink during the Sandhipuja on the night of Ashtami during the Durga Puja—Aritra wished he could dance the same way now to release the joy and thrill, the virility and desire, pent up within himself.

As they climbed the flight of stairs towards the Parvati temple, Neelam sat down on one of the steps. 'What do you think?'

The town of Pune was spread out far below Esha's feet. The winding lines of the river, the bridge, gardens—the water and the road indistinguishable with the sun shining on them. 'Beautiful,' said Esha.

'Really?'

'The truth and nothing but the truth.'

'In court now?'

'Why not? So long as I'm not here to be a false witness.'

'Then let us have your entire testimony.'

'You're very tired, aren't you?'

'Aren't you tired too?'

'I am. The sun's so strong. I didn't realize in the morning how hot it would get. What did you mean, my testimony?'

'Should I speak freely?' asked Neelam. Looking at her in bewilderment, Esha said, 'Of course.'

'But before that, do we look well?'

'All of you look very well.' Esha said without hesitation. 'I came because I want to visit Ajanta. But unless I'd seen your family, especially Pupu, there would have been a gap in my life, Neelam.'

'Tell me the truth, Esha,' said Neelam. 'Are you here only to visit Ajanta? Is that possible? There are other, easier routes to Ajanta. Why did you pick this one?'

Esha said, 'I cannot say what was in my subconscious mind, Neelam. But as far as the conscious mind goes, I'm here so that you and Ari can show me around. I'm not from the West, my experiences of travelling alone have not been pleasant.'

After some hesitation, Neelam asked, 'Don't you bear any grudges, any regrets?'

Suddenly Esha laughed. Neelam's hair was flying. Tucking them behind Neelam's ears, Esha said, 'Believe me, there's no passion left in me—neither rage nor love. I couldn't have come if either had remained. Could you have? Tell me.'

'Please don't mind, Esha. It's just that I have lost so much, the ground beneath my feet is so wobbly, that I get afraid easily. Even if you have no passion left, Ari has all of his.'

'If he does, I promise to throw cold water on it.'

'But you cannot be blamed for bearing a grudge. What happened was utterly unfair to you, which I must admit if I look at it objectively.'

Esha said, 'Emotions cannot be stolen, Neelam. It may be ethically correct to be fair in love, but truth is different, reality is different. Besides, what happened was for the best, Neelam. You know what Ari is like. He would have venerated me as a goddess or something all my life, put me on a pedestal. This is a far more natural outcome. Both of us were saved.'

This hurt Neelam deeply. Was she only a flesh-and-blood woman? Someone who met Aritra's needs, who ran his household for him, while Esha would always be the more valuable one.

She couldn't put it this way. She had already violated the laws of hospitality by asking Esha why she had come. Ari would raise hell if he found out. But the agony, the suffering in her heart refused to die down. She said, 'I'm asking a personal question now, please don't mind. Why did you get divorced? I heard he was the ideal man in every way. Just that he was somewhat older, isn't that so?'

Esha did not answer. When she saw Neelam still looking at her questioningly, she said, 'Don't worry, I didn't do it for Ari.'

'Is that what I said?'

'Not everything can be explained, can it?'

Although Neelam knew she was crossing the bounds of civility, and that Esha would think badly of her, she did not let up. She had disclosed much of her own personal difficulties to Esha in a burst of emotion. Esha too should break her silence and answer.

'You were in the Gulf, weren't you?'

'Yes, Bahrain. Five years.'

'And then?'

'Then I went back to Calcutta.'

'Who else lived there with you?'

'His parents. He. No one else.'

'A nice small family. Did your in-laws trouble you? Did they treat you badly?'

With a sigh Esha said, 'They weren't bad people, Neelam. But my father-in-law treated me like a paid nurse, and my mother-in-law, like her personal maid.'

'So you were being forced to serve your in-laws.'

'No, that's not what it was, Neelam. My father-in-law was very fond of me, he needed me even to fetch him a glass of water. Say the jug was in his room, within arm's reach. And I was having a bath. He wouldn't have a drink of water till I poured him a glass. And my mother-in-law? I had to hear her criticize my family and neighbours for hours on end. I didn't even know all of these people. I had to accompany her to every Hindi and Bangla film she wanted to watch. Sit with her during every TV serial. I used to do all that too, but Neelam, if you're born a human you need some time to yourself, to do your own things. But they just wouldn't allow me that time. I had to divide my entire time, my entire life, between the three of them. Not even my sleep was my own, it used to be interrupted without warning. I insisted on taking my final exam. Surreptitiously I sent off the application that got me a college job. They couldn't accept this.'

'It's sounding most primitive, Esha, not modern at all.'

'So what? A husband and his parents accept dowry, ask for thousands of rupees more, and then kill the bride. That's not modern either, in fact it sounds quite medieval. Doesn't it? But it happens all the time. Many parents get their sons married because they need a high-class maid. It's an eternal idea in our country, Neelam—a man gets married so that his wife can look after his parents. Looking after them is not the issue, that's an aspect of daily life. But how can you look for a wife with the same objective as for a maid or a nurse? Think about it, Neelam. And then, chewing on her paan and zarda, that smile, and her endless criticism of inter-caste love. I wanted to scream.'

'You could have objected.'

'You have no idea, no matter how well-educated you are, no matter how much of an adult you are, expressing your own opinion or taste is completely forbidden. Whenever I tried, I was accused of arrogance and rudeness. I was compared at every step to the woman married to our neighbours. Mind you, she had tried to get friendly with me specifically to badmouth her mother-in-law. She handed over her two children to her in-laws unconditionally to secure her own release from them.'

'You'd have survived if you had children, Esha.'

'I would have died some more, Neelam. I wouldn't have been able to give them the chance to bloom, the one your Pupu has had. My anguish would have been multiplied. Some of us simply cannot suppress our taste, our learning, our personality, no matter how hard we try.'

'But why did your parents pick such a strange family?'

'They didn't seem strange. You cannot make out these things beforehand. My mother-in-law was a college graduate. My father-in-law, a retired judge. So what? Just the one son. And that too was agony. Working out how much of him belonged to me and how much to his parents was a daily battle.'

'Was the son mostly his parents', then?' Neelam's voice was taunting.

'No,' answered Esha briefly.

'Well then? Did he also use you as a goddess?'

'No, he used me as his bathroom.' Esha's face lost colour as soon as she blurted this out. Agony was written so large on her face, a deep sense of shame, sadness and ineffable humiliation had aged her so much at this moment, that Neelam bowed her head. Realizing that she should not have interrogated Esha this way, Neelam felt very sorry. But she had not asked the questions out of feminine inquisitiveness, she needed to know where Esha stood today, what her relationship with Aritra could be like. Knowing in advance would enable her to ward off danger. It was a matter of life and death for her. Esha would forgive her if she understood. Forgive me, Esha. I have been the cause of your suffering earlier too. Great suffering. Even now I continue to torment you. Poor Esha, how downcast you look. Have you gone back to the exhausting memory of giving unwanted company to your former in-laws even though it went against your grain, or perhaps of desire-less cohabitation with your husband? Forgive me for taking you back to your nightmare. You are probably a tiny bird, but even if you are, you die if you cannot swim in the sky. I have understood you a little bit, Esha. And it is because you fly that I dare to ask you for forgiveness again and again.

They had lunch at a small, clean restaurant near the Deccan Gymkhana. Both of them silent. Both of them melancholy. Back home Neelam unlocked the front door, while Esha stood absently next to her. Neelam did not know how deep Esha's despair and depression ran. Every time they hit Esha she exhausted her strength to combat them, expending the last drop of her blood. But she was determined to conquer them. With all her effort she said, I am deep in the heart of darkness, but I am ascending towards the light. The more extreme, the more dense, the more impenetrable the darkness was, the more her resolve grew. The light, the light—eventually she would reach the light, she would. Neelam did not know. But what Neelam could see now in her beautiful portico was a tree felled by lightning. No leaves, the branches fallen off, only a black trunk with the ancient remnants of leaves and boughs on its gnarled surface. Tears streamed from Neelam's eyes. Reaching out, she said, 'Come, Esha, I shall never bring up the past again.'

A mass of clouds were gathering in Esha's sky. These were not Rabindranath's romantic clouds, but Sudhindranath Dutta's cataclysmic ones. With all her strength Esha tried to break out of the vaporous web. Where is the sun, where are you, do not hide your face repeatedly in the vessel of mud. *Tatwam pushan apavrinu jyotidharma drishaye*. Uncover the light so that the seeker may see it.

NINE

Mahanam's lecture was scheduled for the first half of the seminar. Only ten minutes had been allocated for questions and answers, which did not prove sufficient. Several students had surrounded him with their queries during lunch. Answering them offered a pleasant opportunity to expand one's ideas, which Mahanam was enjoying enormously. 'No, you're wrong,' he was saying. 'It isn't a matter of which is better. One art form is bound to attack another, especially if the same artist were to use both. The artist's personality asserts itself, perhaps unknown to him. When Nikhilesh is talking to the village heads in *Home and the World*, the director uses him like a fashion model. He has even arranged the folds of his shawl in perfect layers. Nikhilesh is a little stiff in the scene, as though to maintain the character of a photograph. *Kanchanjangha*, *The Chess Players*, *The Music Room*—all of these are a painter's films, episodic in structure.'

Chandrashekhar came up to Mahanam, telling him that a Swedish student whose research had brought him here wanted to say something. Turning around, Mahanam discovered a young man with thin blond hair and pale eyes looking at him eagerly. He was studying the social background of Satyajit Ray's cinema. Chandrashekhar translated his question. 'In the last sequence of *Home and the World*, Bimala's attire is gradually transformed into a widow's garb. The director has presented this as a great tragedy, as though widowhood itself is a tragedy. But Bimala was bound to Nikhilesh only out of a sense of familial and social responsibility, not through a bond of love. Her relationship with Nikhilesh was like that between a mentor and a disciple. Sandeep may have proved a complete failure, but it was he who had aroused both her mind and body. Would it not have been more realistic for Bimala to prepare for larger and wider experiences now?'

Mahanam said, 'The social context in which Ray's film is set did not allow widowhood to be reversed. And this was considered a curse. No matter how enlightened a woman might be, she did not have the power to bypass this tradition, or to remain completely untouched by it. The methods for breaking socio-religious barriers are completely unknown to her. Bimala has now lost the entire freedom she could enjoy while a husband as broadminded as Nikhilesh was alive. Widowhood was indeed the ultimate tragedy for Bimala.

'The other thing you do not seem to have noticed is the subtle change in the relationship between Nikhil and Bimala. What was originally a traditional relationship between a husband and wife, which Nikhil had wanted to be released from during the Sandeep episode, later moved to the turf of personality clash and love. It's a tragedy of personality and love, not so much for Bimala as for Nikhilesh. This was what Nikhilesh had wanted. This clear-eyed way of seeing things. To establish themselves alongside events in the world and other people, and to understand themselves through comparisons and contrasts. And that is just what happens. But Bimala's lapse during the Sandeep episode caused more pain to Nikhilesh than he could have ever imagined. And so he chooses the path of suicide.'

Johann said, 'Then I must say Nikhilesh is not entirely free of orthodoxy.'

'Of course he's not. We bear orthodoxy in our blood. We can keep it at bay with our intellect, but the moment we are in emotional territory it raises its head.'

'So Nikhilesh punishes Bimala,' said Johann.

'Very perceptive of you. Of course he does. After all, no one knows better than him how strong the socio-religious chains of widowhood are. But it is difficult to say how much of it is conscious. Nikhilesh is in fact the most complex character in the film. His final decision includes the desire to take revenge on Bimala as a spurned lover, the bravado to prove his superiority as a husband over his rival, and even the heartfelt wish as a landowner to take the responsibility for maintaining peace.'

Johann's next question: 'In *Days and Nights in the Forest* Ray depicts another widow, whose husband has committed suicide in a foreign country for some unknown reason, and who now lives with her dead husband's family. In the desolate area of the forest where they live, she offers herself to one of four friends—all strangers to her—visiting them. What prevents the man from accepting her? He has already displayed his interest in the woman. His behaviour now is utterly inhuman. Why doesn't the director show them sleeping together, Godard certainly would have.'

Mahanam smiled. 'Three-fourths of what is observed in the society and culture of our country is accepted by our art. It would be unrealistic otherwise. What is shown in this film is that the physical purity of upper class women in our country cannot be defiled easily, unlike the case of the adivasi woman which is depicted alongside.'

'Not even if the woman wants it?'

'No, not even if the woman wants it. Secondly, the young man is not at all ready to accept the woman, no matter how much he flirts with her. There are certain implications of accepting a woman of her status, which the young man is quite aware of. On top of which, there is his natural inhibition.'

'Why, because she is a widow?'

Mahanam seemed to falter.

Johann said, 'So what you're saying is that, even in the fifty or sixty years since 1905, Indian society has not become remotely progressive about widowhood. This man is selfish, incapable of shouldering a responsibility, which includes sexual impotence.'

'Yes,' agreed Mahanam. 'But had he surrendered to the moment, we would have called him even more selfish.'

'How strange,' said Johann. His pen raced over the pages of his notebook. Heaven knew what sort of trial he would subject Indian society to.

Turning to Chandrashekhar, Mahanam said, 'Do you see how differences in social systems create a gulf of difference in perspectives, Shekhar? That's why they could not accept *The Goddess* despite its being such a good film. Long mental conditioning has come in the way of savouring art. And besides, Shekhar, I think there are some eternal values in human relationships, where we have retained some of the basics.'

'Eternal values? I don't get it,' said Chandrashekhar.

'Take our natural compassion for victims. That's an eternal value, isn't it? But in *Days and Nights in the Forest* we did not view the deprived wife with compassion. She has been treated as an eccentric rather than a pathetic figure.'

'Explain, please.'

'What is *Days and Nights in the Forest*? An excursion into the unfamiliar, the bizarre. Four friends are visiting a secluded forest region as a break from boredom. Nature, the people, and their ways are all unfamiliar to them. Not just unfamiliar, but odd, unsettling. We are being deeply unfair to the widow by considering her a part of this unsettling atmosphere. You understand? We are presenting her natural desire for love as a freak illness. That's why Johann as a human being feels revolted.'

As he left the auditorium, Mahanam remembered his aunt Kasturi, who was married at fourteen and widowed at fifteen. That was when her father came to his senses. He had faithfully performed the task of protecting his daughter from the sympathy of relatives and the possessive love of her property-hungry in-laws, ensuring that she got an education and went abroad. His aunt used to say, 'Not everyone is as lucky.' The foundations of Mahanam's attitude towards people were formed by her. This same aunt died of a sudden heart attack at fifty-five. Without any warning. Whatever other problems she may have had, her heart and brain had always been sound.

She returned from the nursing home in the afternoon, rinsing her hands and arms at the basin, covering them with soap and antiseptic up to the elbows. Her apron hung from a hook in the wall. Yagneshwar brought her some shorbot, grumbling under his breath. A few slices of cucumber, a boiled egg. Some pomegranate and cold milk. This was her afternoon meal. But today she had asked for only a glass of shorbot, which meant she would not eat anything more. Which was why Joggeshwar was infuriated.

'Has anyone ever grown rich on food?' she was asking, laughing. She had sat down on the sofa with the glass. Mahanam was at the other end with his book. Suddenly the glass fell from her hand, shattering on the floor. When he looked up, startled, she said, 'My hand turned numb.' Still grumbling, Joggeshwar said, 'I'll make you another glass at once. Don't fall asleep.' Her sleep was custom made. After her meal she would lean back in the sofa for exactly twenty minutes, silent and still. She knew all the rules of resting. When an hour had passed Mahanam called out to her—'It's time to eat, Kasturi Debi.' She didn't wake up. 'Time to wake up, Mashi.' She didn't wake up. Mahanam nudged her, Kasturi slumped to one side. Mahanam understood at once. It really had been time for her to go.

But how had he felt? As though someone was missing,

something was missing? Here a moment ago, but gone now. An emptiness. How often did he meet his aunt anyway, once he had left the hostel and moved back home? At ten at night, at seven in the morning, and from one to two in the afternoon. They would chat for a while at night. Of late Mahanam had begun to spend those hours with his books. Even if there had been an emptiness, the whirlwind that followed sucked everything in. His aunt's distant relatives opposed her will. The seasoned solicitor from her father's era said, 'Why are you causing trouble, my friends? The cash was all earned by Kasturi Mitra herself, it has long been transferred to Mahanam Roy's account. The house was built with the money earned by Kasturi's father, who had bequeathed it unconditionally to his only child. There's nothing you can touch.'

Then came Trinity College at Oxford, Professor Decker, friends and lovers. There was no time for emptiness. He returned from his sojourn abroad four years later, after travelling through all of Europe. The same Joggeshwar, the same marble floor with black and white squares. Wardrobes with enormous mirrors, walls with mouldings, chandeliers. Under the chandeliers, crowds of students.

They thronged to him in large numbers. Esha wasn't supposed to be among them. She was new to the college, studying in the undergraduate classes. But she didn't consider her rights any less than anyone else's. Mahanam could not get away with ambiguous statements. Why weren't 'smooth as silk' or 'hammer and tongs' considered clichés? Why shouldn't 'a mile of peace and quiet' or 'as swift as the legs of a deer' be considered mixed metaphors?

What sort of comparison was 'people worked in a group like election ballots'? Couldn't the phrase 'nature's boudoir' have been avoided? She posed questions like these with an expression that suggested they were matters of life and death.

Poetry searched for its own articulation in a frenzy, it was pervaded by subtle irony from time to time, it was busy trying to awaken its slumbering audience with bursts of flippancy concealed in its gravity, it inevitably considers the vocabulary of its own language insufficient and acquires words from all known languages—Mahanam had devoted his time to explaining all this to her. He had to promise to help her read world literature. Or else Esha grew miserable.

Suddenly Mahanam asked, 'Your friend, that boy. How is he?'

'He's very well.'

'That's a myth. He's not very well at all. A ragged philosopher, doesn't comb his hair, wears rumpled clothes, he's a sulphur patient.'

TEN

Chandrashekhar was going into town for his survey, he would be there all day. He dropped Mahanam on his way. 'You won't find Chowdhury at home unless you get there early,' he had said. 'Though I'm not sure whether he has rejoined his office yet.' Mahanam would have preferred to have gone in the evening. Visiting people at home in the morning meant bothering them. But there might be other guests in the evening, and Mahanam felt no urge to meet anyone, especially strangers, besides Aritra and Neelam. Even Chandrashekhar had said, 'They might be calling on someone in the evening, the Chowdhury couple is extremely sociable.' Mahanam bid Chandrashekhar goodbye on the main road. He walked around the corner, as though this was the preface to the main story or article. Savouring this preface, Mahanam came to a halt in front of the B block. It was Saturday, nearly 8.30 in the morning. He had rushed to get hold of Aritra Chowdhury. He wished he had more time. There was a small lawn in front of the house. Three wicker chairs, a stool, and a folding table of steel. A cushion lying on the grass. There must have been crumbs on the ground, for several crows were pecking away. Ari Chowdhury was the perfect householder, he took care of cats and crows too. Mahanam surveyed the entire house. Some birds had built nests here, having flown from one horizon to another, from one sanctuary to another. He needn't have come. A few questions answered, mysteries unravelled . . . but could all questions even be answered? Mahanam was not vain enough to presume he could solve every mystery in his life. Since it concerned the human factor rather than mathematics. Possibly the birds were thinking of him as a falcon or owl or something equally predatory. Let them—he had no wish at this moment to inform them that he was nothing of the kind. What was wrong with a little apprehension, a little infatuation? It wasn't bad at all. Till such time as one could become truly free of attachment, anger, fear and rage, a little anxiety in daily life was useful. Else the level of anarchy rose. Climbing up the two steps leading to the veranda, Mahanam pressed the bell next to the maroon door. Barely had it rung when the door opened. Esha stood before him. Dressed in a sky-blue sari with white dots, and a thin black shawl, tucking in wisps of hair that had escaped on either side of her face, she opened the door of Aritra's house. Mahanam had never had a bigger surprise in his life. Esha stood facing him, silent with wonder. Neither Neelam nor Aritra had remembered to tell her that Mahanam was here. They had been busy with Esha herself, so busy that they had even forgotten the momentous news of Mahanam's arrival. Aritra might even have secretly hoped that Mahanam would not show up.

'Dare I believe my eyes?' said Mahanam. 'You *are* Esha?'

'So it seems.'

'Not a doppelganger? Or a twin I didn't know about? Like they have in the movies . . .'

Esha laughed. Mahanam had placed one foot inside the room. 'I'm not part of a science fiction story, am I?' he said. 'The gates of this house don't lead back to 1969, do they? O woman, if thou art Esha, how couldst thou appear as the Esha of the 1970s in 1988 without science fiction . . .'

Esha said, 'I'm tired of hearing this, Mahanam-da. Those who keep moving cannot be touched by time easily, it loses the race to them, and besides, you haven't changed much either.'

Touching his sideburns and running his hand through his beard pointedly, Mahanam said, '*Thodi daari pakka, thodi aur kachha, wohi aadmi sachha, wohi aadmi sachha*. Salt and pepper in his hair, that's the man whose heart is clear. Now tell me what's going on. The other night it was Neelam who came out, and this morning it's you. Has Aritra married both of you, then?'

Unable to contain herself, Esha laughed loudly. The sound of the laughter reached the bathroom, from which Aritra emerged in surprise. He had been shaving, a towel draped around his shoulders. Neelam came out of the kitchen with a tin of spices in her hand, and Pupu from the study, parting the curtains.

Mahanam towered over everyone on this side of the room. A giant of a man in a sparkling white kurta-pyjama. And then there was Pupu on the other side, almost as tall as her father. An extraordinary young woman five feet nine inches of height.

'Perfect,' said Mahanam. 'Your clarion call has brought all the actors out one by one, Esha. Three of the faces are familiar to me, though I'm having to strain my eyes a little to recognize some of them. Introduce me to the fourth.'

Putting his arm around Pupu, practically encircling her, Aritra said, 'This is Pupu. Samidhha Chowdhury. My only child. She's studying architecture. Pupu, this is the famous Dr Mahanam Roy. History, sociology, literature, art, mathematics—I'm not entirely sure which of them is actually his subject. You could call him the Aristotle of modern India, although he knows very little about your subject.'

Pupu was staring at Mahanam in surprise. Neelam could see her staring, Mahanam could see that Neelam had turned pale.

Pupu greeted Mahanam, saying, 'Have I met you somewhere, professor? I must have.'

Mahanam said, 'Did you by any chance go to the lectures at the film institute or at Max Müller Bhavan last week? I don't think that's likely.'

'No, but I have never seen a face so familiar. Excuse me, I'm going to the market.' Pupu seemed to be talking in a trance.

'I'm ready,' said Esha. 'Just a minute, let me get the shopping bags. We'll be back soon Mahanam-da, don't go away.'

Entering the kitchen to get the bags, Esha found Neelam weeping silently. Weeping while she pretended to wash the dishes at the sink. Fat tears fell from her eyes, soaking everything.

'What's this Neelam, what are you doing?' whispered Esha. 'Don't cry, everything will be all right.'

Hurrying out through the back door, Esha sat pillion behind Pupu on the scooter, which sputtered around the side of the house and rolled down the slope leading away from the portico outside the open front door. At top speed, Pupu sat in front, in trousers and a baggy shirt, her hair cut short, astonishment frozen in her wide eyes, frowning slightly. She was holding the handles tightly, as though determined not to let them slip out of her grasp. Pupu was going away to a distant land on a winged horse. The sorceress sat behind her, having promised to help her in a crisis. Would Pupu need help?

Aritra said a little belligerently, 'Please sit down, Mahanam-da. How long do you want to keep standing?'

Taking a seat, Mahanam asked directly, 'Is she mine?'

Aritra was reddening. Contemptuously he said, 'The seed might be yours, but she's my daughter.'

'I've never seen such an uncanny resemblance,' said Mahanam. 'It's like looking at myself in the mirror. Did Neelam think about me all the time during her pregnancy? If that were so why did she go away?'

Emerging from the kitchen, Neelam said, 'Suppose the girl IS yours. Are you going to uproot her and take her away, or will you shout it from the rooftops? Which of these do you want?'

'Just a minute. Everything's become entangled. Let me unravel the knots one by one. So you are virtually admitting that she's mine. Aritra has brought her up for so many years, with so much affection, that he could easily say that the seed may be mine but the daughter is his. In other words, he has been a loving father. I can tell by looking at you that you're happy, Neelam, in fact there has been an excess of happiness. No, I will certainly not take Samiddha away, but she is an expression of myself. I don't think anyone who sees the two of us together will have the slightest doubt about whose child she is. Alas, Aritra, it appears that the lord has played a massive joke on you. And you're bearing the joke like a fool. Why have you dressed her like a boy? The resemblance is even more obvious.'

'She prefers to dress this way,' said Neelam succinctly.

Mahanam said, 'Thankfully she doesn't have a beard, that's the only saving grace. Now what is the way out?'

'The only way out is for you to leave,' said Aritra curtly. 'The sooner the better. Leave Pune.'

Shaking his head, Mahanam said, 'Once upon a time you did not observe the courtesy of a guest, today you aren't observing the duty of a host either. I expected as much, more or less. But what you're saying isn't possible, Aritra. I have a fixed schedule, I cannot inconvenience myself for the sake of your small convenience. But I'd better not appear among your acquaintances. They have invited me to a literary meet for Bengalis, I'll tell Shekhar to turn them down. But where did Esha come from? All my lost treasures seem to be in your grasp. By what magic? Have you turned into a yaksha or something?'

'There must be some magic,' said Aritra, 'which is beyond you.'

The doorbell rang, and Aritra hurried to open the door. It was the lady from the flat upstairs. The bulb in the passage was fused, she had something to say about it.

At once Mahanam turned his back on her and became very busy stuffing his pipe with tobacco. When the lady had left he turned to Neelam with a smile. 'One can't see one's back. Can you check whether I look like Samiddha from the back?'

Resuming his seat, Aritra said, 'Yes, it's important to consider what people will think. But your moustache and beard will make the resemblance less obvious. I'm thinking of Pupu. What if she guesses?'

Neelam, who had been sitting with her head in her hands, said, 'That's what I was thinking too.'

Mahanam said, 'There's not much to think about. She knows already.'

Neelam's face was drained of colour 'What do you mean?' she asked.

'Nonsense!' exclaimed Aritra, agitated.

'I know what I'm saying. Samiddha knows that she has a deep relationship with me. She's not only extremely intelligent, her intuition is mature too. I have created a miracle. Aritra, I hope you will not prevent me from enjoying, not my right, but the joy of such creation.'

Neelam gazed steadily at Mahanam. His sideburns had greyed a little, so had his hair and beard. A man of unusually powerful build. And yet his eyes were big and distant. His most prominent feature was his nose. Thin, fragile, not like a human's. It was this nose and those eyes that had captivated Neelam. Her mother had deposited her at the hostel. Her local guardian was her mother's friend's son. Dubbed Aristotle by students, part mockingly, part reverentially. Neelam Joshi couldn't sleep nights unless she visited Mahanam-da every day for Aristotelian wisdom.

Those were the days of shoreless seas. How long had it taken Mahanam to identify the besotted creature? Women themselves didn't know the weapons they used in different ways to enchant the man of their desires. Neelam had wielded all of them, holding nothing back. Her quiver held as many arrows as her ten hands did missiles. Smiles flowered on intimate summer afternoons. The skilled archer struck every target in her body with his arrows. Surrender in her breath. If Mahanam was absorbed in her, Neelam lost herself completely, entranced, mesmerized. Mahanam had not hypnotized her knowingly, Neelam's fate had played this game with her. Two enchantments were bound to lead to the ultimate union. Neelam could still see two enormous eyes poised over her face, the nostrils flared, suddenly Mahanam's mouth descends on hers. This way, exactly this way, Pupu was conceived, amidst entrancement and captivation, although it was doubtful whether Pupu's own personality had the ability to be enchanted.

Seeing Neelam shiver, Aritra said, 'It's chilly, Neelam, use a cotton shawl or something.'

'Who knows whether she's shivering with cold or trembling in delight, Ari,' said Mahanam, smiling.

Aritra looked grim. Mahanam was trying to prove that no matter how anxious Neelam's husband might be for her health, he knew her more intimately.

'I'll get you a cup of tea, Mahanam-da,' said Neelam,

springing to her feet. 'You must have lunch with us today.'

Mahanam said, 'I had an enormous breakfast, with two or three cups of tea. No more tea for me, Neelam. All right, make me a light lemon tea.'

Aritra was surprised. Neelam had invited Mahanam of her own accord, without even checking with him—the same Mahanam whose name could well turn out to be Mahakal, or death. Having lunch meant spending a long time here. Esha would return, they would chat, Pupu would return, would Mahanam chat with her too? Not only was Saturday ruined, but there would now be a layer of anxiety on top of it.

'Play some music, Aritra,' said Mahanam.

'Why this sudden desire for music?'

Laughing, Mahanam said, 'When discomfited hosts have nothing to say and feel the need to conceal this foolish silence with words, they usually put on some music. Jagjit Singh or Ghulam Ali or Anup Jalota or whatever you like. Guzzle on ghazals, or give us a vision of bhajans.'

'Are you taunting me, Mahanam-da?' asked Aritra hotly. 'I've long gone past the age of tolerating taunts.'

Mahanam said, 'Look my friend, if it comes to that, the relationship between us is such that we could easily fight a French duel. My exercise chart will tell you what the outcome will be. Even without the chart, my physique alone makes it clear. But there's no need for all that. Do you know where philosophers triumph over poets? Philosophers can see through poets clearly when they try to win women over with flattery. I shan't lie, if you hold on to Neelam, not even the most adroit thief can take her away. But you have a big problem, for you resort to lies far too often. Poets already have the licence to tell enchanting untruths, but by resorting to much lower lies you have proved yourself worthy of my hatred. What did you tell Neelam to keep her from trusting me even in her crisis? Look, Aritra, I don't like considering a rival as a hateful person, can't you help me get rid of my loathing? I'm too old to live with hatred now.'

Trying his utmost to restrain himself, Aritra said, 'Are you demanding an explanation about Neelam? After all these years? Because you were my teacher once and I gained considerably as a result, I'm not responding to your insult. Any further and we'll have to go to court.'

Mahanam said, 'It's defamation only when the accusation is false. You know very well that I told the truth about your lying. You used a heap of lies to snatch Neelam away from me, and another pile of falsehoods to prevent Esha from getting closer to me. What exactly were these lies?'

Aritra said angrily, 'You're so full of yourself that you know nothing about yourself. Do you know how everyone in our circle referred to you? As a womanizer. You hear me? A dirty womanizer. You seduced women serially with your hoax of knowledge and wisdom and learning. No matter how much pleasure you may have derived from considering yourself a Don Juan, the licentiousness of Oxford was not acceptable in the Calcutta of the seventies. If I had revealed the details of the Neelam episode you would have been murdered by Naxalites.'

Mahanam listened calmly. When Aritra was done

he said, 'Incredible! Despite the presence of a talented lover of women like yourself, the members of your circle identified me as the womanizer? Most peculiar. That was why you delivered several long lectures on the subject of this aspect of my character, didn't you? Now the knots are being unravelled. But as far as I know Esha wanted you, why did you discard her just to deprive me? And even after this, when Esha came to my door in ignominy and condemnation after getting no sympathy from her supremely conservative family, you didn't forget to fire your secret arrow on that occasion either. You used Neelam to pluck Esha out, then used Esha to . . . No, Aritra, it isn't clear to me just how you used them. Your chemistry is most unusual.'

Neelam had slipped out through the back door to get lemons. Now she put the lemon tea down on the table and left. She realized that Mahanam and Aritra were having a showdown, which was necessary. It had been pending for a long time.

Aritra noticed with surprise that he was not as angry as he should have been. He had been throwing his darts accurately. The goddess of victory was on his side. Suddenly breaking into a laugh, he said, 'You've hurled all these obscene accusations at me. But it is still in MY kitchen that Neelam is cooking for you, and Esha welcomed you to MY house before going shopping for you.'

Mahanam laughed loudly. 'Good! Finally you've become an adult, Aritra. This is what I always told you. You need maturity—in intelligence, as in emotion. If you can place your heart and your head in a vertical line, your knowledge will be liberated and your liberation will be knowledgeable. *Sa Vidya Ya Vimuktaye*. Knowledge liberates. Good. I'm not the least bit angry with you.'

Esha and Pupu returned at this moment. Their faces were red from the sun. Aritra said peremptorily, 'How many times have I told you to use a cap, Pupu? Esha, you could have covered your head. The sun is very strong. I have no idea how you will go to Aurangabad in this weather. Ellora is a hard journey in any case. What do you think, Mahanam-da?'

'For now I think nothing. Let's get there first. I HAVE to go.'

Esha sat down. 'Go where? To Ellora? Are you going, Mahanam-da? Come with us then. We're . . . at least, I'm definitely going. Why do you say you HAVE to go?'

'For something I'm writing,' said Mahanam. 'But unless I know what your plans are . . .'

Coming into the room, Neelam said, 'Whatever the plans might be, you're definitely going with them.'

'Are you going to write on art, Dr Roy?' asked Pupu.

Mahanam turned to her. 'What would you like me to write on?'

'Art and religion,' answered Pupu.

'All right,' said Mahanam, 'that's what I'll write on. Can you read Bangla?'

'Not very well,' said Pupu, sounding embarrassed.

'This isn't right, Neelam. Bangla is not only her mother tongue but also a beautiful language in its own right. You're wrong not to have taught her. Non-Bengalis who live in West Bengal can all read and write their mother tongues.'

Pupu said, 'The fault is mine. I did learn it, but I've forgotten out of lack of use. I'll make up for it. Will you write in Bangla?'

Mahanam did not tell her that this was part of a book he was planning. Commissioned by a foreign publisher. All he said absently was, 'Since you're saying you'll brush up your Bangla, Samidhha, I'll write it in Bangla and send it to you. But why are you so concerned with the relationship between art and religion?'

'I was wondering whether art could be interpreted as a kind of religion,' said Pupu. 'My mother has a religion, Dr Roy, she puts flowers in front of idols in that room, incense, water from the river—she uses these and prays to those images. My mother often has altercations with my father. He says, why do you keep talking about sinning? Sin is a mental illness, and piety is mental health. The most effective way to preserve mental health is catharsis, which means doing whatever you want to, within limits. And if you want to attain peace through concentration, then read, paint, sculpt, write poetry. Now what I want to know is the relationship between my mother's rituals and my father's. I feel it is of vital importance to me.'

Aritra looked at Neelam. They had indeed argued over these things now and then, but they hadn't imagined even in their dreams that Pupu had listened eagerly and that she could convey the essence of their debate so succinctly and in such a composed manner to everyone.

Mahanam was astonished. For some reason his eyes glowed with joy. He said, 'What do you think of religion? Do you have one, Pupu?'

'I do, Dr Roy. Let's say I concentrate on books, or on my drawing. I have some rituals too, which I use to recover my mental health—exercising, listening to music, going to art exhibitions and galleries. I make it a point to give something to someone every day, Dr Roy. I cannot tell you how it makes me feel deep inside, it must be a ritual.'

Pupu's parents were amazed. What she was saying today was about her inner life. She had never talked about it before. Never discussed it. Nor had she asked questions. Aritra felt hurt. Neelam was happy, she didn't know why. Esha wanted to give Pupu a big kiss, she didn't know why either. Love tried to flow towards the 18-year-old girl in a thousand different streams.

Mahanam smiled. 'Five hundred years before Christ was born, at the time of Pericles in Athens, imagine an evening symposium being held at the farmhouse of a gentleman named Phaedo or Xenophone. Several young men of your age are present, Samiddha, though there isn't a single young woman. Let's take you to the gathering as the only lady in attendance.'

'Socrates would be there, wouldn't he?' said Pupu. 'And Plato? Whose role will you play there, Dr Roy? Will it be Plato's?'

Mahanam said, 'Absolutely not. I am a curious young man, I could have any name, Euripides, for instance.'

Suddenly Neelam interjected, 'What's all this Dr Roy business, Pupu? Is this any way to address such a great man? I don't get the culture of your generation.'

'What should I call him then?' Pupu accepted her

mother's reprimand like a little girl. 'Should I call him "uncle"?'

Mahanam burst into laughter. 'Let her not call me by any name at all, Neelam, instead of "uncle". What's wrong with "Dr Roy"?'

ELEVEN

Like a giant swan, the milky white car glided around the corner in Priyalkarnagar, the light bouncing off its body. Its slow, silent movement was regal. But seeing it sent shivers down the spine. The car was unfamiliar, but Neelam had not the slightest of doubt that it was Bikram's. He never kept a car very long, and two of them were always available for the husband's and the wife's independent use. Bikram changed his own car frequently. The Standard Herald that Seema used had probably been with her for the past ten years. It was Bikram's first car. This one must be his latest acquisition. Looked like a Contessa. Who knew whether Seema was inside or not. Neelam opened the door and went out into the portico. Her wet hair had dried now, and was fixed in place with a clip. Since Esha's arrival Neelam had been dressing in saris all day long, slipping on an apron while cooking. A pale pink Tangail sari today—Neelam had dressed modestly.

Seema's face was visible in the window. 'Hel . . . lo!'

She jumped out of the car. 'Do you recognize my dress, Neelam-di?'

'Should I?' asked Neelam.

'Of course. You gave it to me six or seven years ago as a Puja gift.'

An olive green satin weave cascading diagonally downwards in pleats from the left shoulder against magenta silk fabric, with gold embroidery on it. The leggings were two-toned too.

Neelam remembered getting an identical outfit for Pupu, but in black and white. Pupu used to love it, wearing it so often that it had frayed. Astonished, she said, 'Seven years, I think. How well you've preserved it.'

Seema said, 'The dresses from the year before, the year before that, and even the year before that are all as good as new. Why would they be spoilt if I took good care of them? It's so lovely. I used to wear it to parties, now I use it for long journeys.' Seema sounded very pleased with herself. 'You look terrific, Neelam-di. Where's this sari from—is it from Rajkot?'

'Uh-huh. Tangail.'

'Tangail? Really? I just couldn't tell. So fine. Where did you get it?'

'My friend who's visiting us got it for me,' said Neelam.

Bikram was flaunting a wide tie. His naturally fair complexion was accentuated, his cheeks so red that they seemed about to bleed. 'What's going on, Seal sahib?' said Neelam. 'You do seem to be turning into an Englishman.'

Wiping her face with a handkerchief, Seema said,

'Nonsense, that's the colour of alcohol. Gives you a sheen at first, then, as soon as the liver's affected, turns you into an African.'

Bikram had stopped the car. Now, reversing it to park, he said in his deep voice, 'I'm warning you, don't bring up the liver. But Bhabi, your house is supposed to be spilling over with guests, how come you're standing here alone like the bride after the wedding night?'

Bikram got out of the car, slapping the dust off his hands.

Neelam said, 'Spilling over? When did I say that? Just the one guest.'

'But that one guest is as good as twenty more. Bikram Seal is capable of reading as much between the lines. You wouldn't have summoned your servant if it had only been some meek and purring kitten, would you? This one must be a tigress.' Leaping on to the portico, Bikram adopted a tigress pose with his arms spread out.

Looking at him out of the corner of her eyes, Seema said, 'I don't know whether Neelam-di's friend is a tigress, but I have no doubt that you're a sheep in wolf's clothing.'

Bikram walked up to Neelam in pretended rage, saying, 'Tell your friend or sister or whatever she is to withdraw that statement, Bhabi, else there will be a terrible fight, wolves are very low creatures.'

Smothering her laughter, Neelam said, 'Whom will you fight with—Seema or me?'

'Fight with you?' His face suffused with a smile, Bikram said, 'Oh Bhabi, those are just lovers' tiffs. *Manbhanjan, Jaidev, Geetgovindam*. Am I going to be so lucky?'

It was a lovely day. The sun had not yet become

scorching. There was a thin layer of clouds. The sunlight was bright but benign.

Rounding the corner, Aritra's scooter came to a stop. 'Get off, Esha,' said Aritra, 'you don't have to take the bags. I'll be back in a minute from the shop round the corner.'

'Cigarettes?'

Aritra nodded, smiling. Then he turned around and disappeared. Bikram said, 'Did Chowdhury-da beat a retreat at my sight, Bhabi?'

Esha had got off the scooter. She went to the market with Pupu every morning. This morning Ari had demanded that she should go with him to buy chicken. A grown-up throwing a tantrum. It seemed Esha only chatted with Neelam, with Pupu. Didn't Ari exist? Was he just a hanger-on?

Neelam had said, 'My god! Just the other night you drove nine or ten miles with her alone from the station to Priyalkarnagar, you even got rid of the party-pooper Patil, and you still have things to tell her in private?'

Everyone had laughed. Pupu too.

'I'll never run out of things to tell her,' Ari had glowered.

'Mashi, look at him, he's pouting,' Pupu had said. 'He's changing colour. Absolutely green now with jealousy. Do something, Mashi. It's too pathetic a sight to bear.'

Esha said, 'All right. But I won't have anything to do with the chicken. I must be kept at a safe distance.'

Esha didn't eat meat at all. But she loved cooking. She had promised to cook something special on Sunday. Esha threw a glance at Neelam. 'We'll be back as soon as possible, Neelam, don't worry.'

'No, not that way.' Ari was still upset.

'Now what?'

'She has to dress up. A golden silk sari. Fancy hair-do. All the cosmetics you people use.'

'You're not making it easy. My golden silk sari is in a mess. Not ironed, I'd worn it on the train.' Esha left.

She emerged exactly ten minutes later, in an off-white sari without a border, a black bindi on her forehead and a loose bun on her head. Transparent pearl earrings. Light lipstick.

Bikram saw her in the same garb. A juicy cream roll. Sweet filling inside, mouth-watering aroma. Baked lightly by the sun, with great expertise. A perfect salad with Thousand Island dressing. Crisp chin. A nose like a cheese straw, lips like tiny Nagpur oranges. Oysters in the earlobes, cream puff cookies on her cheeks. And, all told, a long strip of succulent golden bacon soft-fried in butter.

'Let me introduce you,' said Neelam. 'This is Bikram Seal. The No. 1 building and road contractor in Bombay. And this is his fortunate wife Seema. As both of you know, this is our friend Esha Khan.'

'Both of yours?' asked Seema with wide eyes. Neelam smiled uncomfortably. Aritra had appeared behind Seema, saying, 'Age cannot wither her, nor custom stale her infinite variety.' Looking suspiciously at Bikram, he added, 'When did you get here?'

Smiling widely, Bikram said, 'Don't worry, Dada, we've only just arrived. I haven't had the chance for any mischief yet.' Turning to Esha, he said, 'You see, Esha-ji, wherever Bikram goes, his reputation precedes him. And once Bikram arrives, all the other gentlemen recede to the background.' Thrusting his chest out, he continued, 'Which is why all these dainty men don't like me at all.' Throwing his arms skywards he sang: "The bandits have been sent, like a roaring torrent."'

'What a lovely voice,' exclaimed Esha spontaneously.

Tilting his head, Bikram looked at Aritra and laughed. 'Did you see Dada, did you see Bhabi, how I won the first round so easily? I come, I see, I conquer.'

Ignoring him completely, Aritra asked Seema, 'How are you, Seemachalam?'

'Me!' said Seema. 'How do you think? I'm in the grips of this evil planet for life. I have no news of my own.' Turning to Bikram, she said, 'We should get our things in order first, shouldn't we?'

Bikram waved her away. 'That's your job, you can do it. I'm going to hold court now with Neelam Bhabi on one side and Esha-ji on the other, while Chowdhury-da stares greedily.'

Everyone except Ari produced a laugh at this. Bikram had started his business enterprise in Pune, where he had arrived with a little capital and some experience. Aritra had helped him a lot to secure orders. His pleasant, sociable nature endeared him to everyone. At that time Bikram and Seema were part of Aritra's shopping expeditions, Neelam's meetings and events, going to the cinema, short holidays, everything. Bikram had practically brought Pupu up. But Aritra felt, in fact he was convinced, that Bikram had not honoured the faith they had reposed in him. Trying to gauge Neelam's involvement in this made him knit his brows. The passage between his heart and lungs felt constricted, so he preferred not to think about it. If Neelam hadn't shielded Bikram, Aritra had considered publicly humiliating him and severing all connections. But he couldn't. One big reason was Pupu. Seema too was a sweet, innocent woman, anyone would think twice before hurting her. Bikram's business had expanded so much that his main office had moved to the suburbs of Bombay. He had a palatial house in Thane. But he hadn't sold his flat in Pune, where he had bought the land at the same time as Aritra. He had a flat in D1, just a few blocks away, with a caretaker in place. He stayed there when he came to Poona, which was quite often.

Seema had picked up a suitcase, with the keys in the other hand, and slung a heavy bag over her shoulder. Aritra said, 'Let me walk you to your flat, Seemachal.'

Looking at him gratefully, Seema said, 'There's no need, Ari-da, really.'

'That's impossible, Seema. I'm told Burma and China have a tradition of women carrying loads, but we have different practices.' Assuming he had delivered a palpable blow, Aritra snatched the suitcase from Seema's hand.

Bikram burst into laughter. 'Abuse me as much as you like, Dada, but Bikram Seal is not budging. I earn millions for her, drove her all the way here. Carry her load too? Can't do so much.'

'Come, Seema,' said Ari, putting his hand on her shoulder.

Seema was slim, petite, nondescript features, a little

puffy. She dressed flawlessly, having apparently mastered every secret of looking attractive from the top beauty parlours of Bombay and Pune. She was articulate, without any inhibitions. Only, Aritra thought of her as a colourful bubble which could burst any moment. So fragile, inflated with so much emptiness. He had never felt the urge to get to know Seema well enough to understand whether the emptiness was in her nature or her experiences. Ari put his hand on her shoulder with great affection. A slender shoulder, which might break under the slightest pressure. How could Bikram let her go off with the suitcase? He was a beast. How could he make her suffer so much? Not a beast, he was a monster.

'What are you thinking about with such concentration, Ari-da?' asked Seema.

'Nothing in particular. Have you informed the caretaker?'

'We don't have a separate caretaker these days. Mohan, the common guard of D1, has a set of keys. We phoned him yesterday, he will have cleaned the flat by now. Your flat's small, you could send Esha-di to ours if you like. There's an entire spare bedroom.'

'Of course not,' said Aritra in panic. Then, calming down a bit, he said, 'Esha is visiting us. What will she think if we pack her off to your flat? There's no need. And I've contacted the MTDC—we're planning to leave tomorrow or the day after.'

'Where are you going? Who's going?'

They had reached Seema and Bikram's flat. Climbing to the first floor and unlocking the door, Seema grew quite cheerful. 'Give me a minute Ari-da, I need to talk to Mohan.'

Seema returned soon. Aritra saw a shadow on her face. 'Did you know Bikram has been here recently, Ari-da?' she asked.

'No, I didn't,' Aritra said. 'He didn't visit us. I didn't see him anywhere either.'

'Mohan says he was here.'

Aritra could sense Seema's throat was dry. She walked across the hall quickly, opening the bedroom door. She was standing with her back to Ari, looking like a very fragile and helpless young girl. What was she looking for? Would Bikram have left any evidence? What if he had? Could Seema do anything about it?

'What are you doing, Seemachal?' asked Aritra. 'Are you going to unpack now? I can help you.'

With her back still turned to him, Seema said, 'No, I'll do it myself. Everything's all right. Let me check the kitchen.'

Seema took a tour of the kitchen. She was restless. 'You'd better go back Ari-da,' she said, 'your friend's here. I'll do whatever little needs to be done here.'

Aritra felt a wave of sympathy. 'I'm in no hurry,' he told her. 'We'll go back together. You can't have much to do here, finish it off quickly and have a cup of tea with Neelam. You must be thirsty.'

Opening the wardrobe, Seema arranged the clothes. Mohan had packed the fridge with liquor. Tinned food too. Seema made some coffee quickly, surprising Ari with a steaming cup. Putting it down in front of him, she said, 'Actually it's you who's thirsty, Ari-da.'

'Aren't you?'

'Very. This coffee won't quench my thirst, Ari-da,' Seema said in a strange voice.

'Oh, I forgot.' She went back into the kitchen and emerged with a plate of biscuits.

'Have some biscuits with your coffee, Ari-da, it's not right to drink coffee without any food. Now tell me who's going on this trip, and where you're going.'

'We're probably taking the night bus to Aurangabad tomorrow. Early in the morning we'll take the tourism board bus there. Two days. The first at Ajanta, the second at Ellora. That's the plan right now. Esha and I are going, so is an old professor of ours, Dr Roy, who's also in Pune right now.'

'Isn't Neelam-di going? Pupu?'

'No. Neelam isn't going because of Pupu's exams. She has her semester exams.'

'If you're off tomorrow, why did you send for us?' complained Seema.

'I'm not sure what Neelam had in mind. But we'll be back in two days. You and Bikram could come along too.'

'But how will we get tickets? Let's go back and tell him at once, then.'

Aritra felt himself on the horns of a dilemma. He did not have the slightest desire to take Bikram along. But nor was it possible to leave his home and household in Bikram's hands again.

Aritra began to fidget. Suppressing the feeling as much as possible, he said, 'If it's going to take you some time more, Seema, I'll go now.' Getting to his feet, he added, 'Come quickly.'

Seema shut the door after Aritra had left. The hall was packed with expensive objects. A chandelier in the centre, casting its light on the revolving bookcase with the encyclopaedia, and on the statue or plants set against each of the walls. Low sofas scattered around the room. Three-legged tables with surfaces resembling brass trays from Moradabad. At first glance the house would be mistaken for the home of an art enthusiast. But the owner was not a connoisseur at all. The owner's wife didn't understand art either. The interior decorator who had done up the flat had fulfilled her own unmet desires. With time hanging heavy on her hands, Seema had also been taking a course in interior decoration. But while she was busy with her course, it provided Bikram a golden opportunity to stray. So Seema had given up her course midway to settle herself back at home.

She found herself crying. Tears streamed from her eyes, her heart ached. But she hadn't realized it. She had discovered some things in the bedroom that had brought fresh confirmation of her husband's infidelity. Mohan would disclose nothing even at the pain of death. What he had revealed was inadvertent.

Going into the bathroom, Seema washed her face with imported soap at the pink basin. Covering her face with foam, she opened her eyes slightly to look at herself in the mirror. In the glow of the pink tiles and the soft light, the foam-covered face in the mirror looked like it was part of a dream. Rinsing the foam would reveal an incredible, enchanting, exquisite woman with a commanding personality, a signal from whose eyes made worlds break up and join again. Everyone knew of them, Seema too. Cleopatra, Noor Jehan, even Mata Hari. Seema thought of them every time she used soap. Slowly, reluctantly, she rinsed her face, observing the emergence of a disappointed girl.

Her brother was sitting on the tree, throwing guavas down and saying, 'Catch, Seema.' A little later she said, 'I want to climb the tree too.'

Her brother said, 'Hmmph! You! Stay where you are.' Seema had become exhausted seeing her brother, just two years older, always perched higher than her. A constant sense of inferiority in her head. As though her brother was always on a pedestal, the giver, and she, eternally lower, the recipient. When she tried to force her way on to the tree, she was bitten by ants, her legs swelling. Her brother said, 'Will you dare climb my tree again? Ever again? Never forget your limits.' Seema's father would visit on the weekend. Or leave on a train. Higher than the ground. Much higher than Seema. Arriving from a distance, going away into the distance. Out of reach.

She was safe as long as her father or brother was near her. There was nothing to be afraid of. No one could harm her. With Bikram next to her, too, Seema was a mere atom. She would have to accept whatever he did, without protesting. Or else she could be flung far, far out of her security net. A great fear. How strange Bikram was. He used to be a music teacher in a small town, singing in his generous voice at local soirees and being invited by neighbours. He started by supplying sand from Magra to builders. Neither the lorry nor the sand was his own. He would talk his way into getting contracts, without any assets of his own. Then, summoning courage, the Bombay Mail with Seema alongside. Incredible determination, boldness, abilities. Seema graduated from Bombay University, did a course in nutrition in Pune, a beautician's course too, but she could not match Bikram's prowess. She did get the prince she had dreamt of in her childhood, but an eternal question mark remained over the last episode of the fairy-tale where they were supposed to have lived happily ever after. This made Seema hysterical at times, forcing her to tear out her hair, such pain, such discomfort, spreading across her body and her mind. Bikram didn't even keep their son at home. First he had the boy admitted to a boarding school in Ooty, and now, in distant Dehradun.

Locking the door of the flat, Seemachal treaded darkness in daylight to walk like a spirit, her eyes guided only by the lights in Ari-da's house. How happy Neelam-di was. How nice Ari-da was. So much affection, caring, compassion. Ari-da had always loved her. From the time they used to live in Pune, next to one another. Ari-da had not become as successful as he was now, nor had Bikram. Ari-da had cared for her like his own sister ever since then. Today all of them were chatting together. Bikram's neglect was palpable. Amidst this humiliation, Ari-da had accompanied her with the suitcase, sat with her in the flat. Did he understand Seema's sadness? Even if he did, he didn't say it. He only wanted to wipe it away with fondness and feeling. Seema felt all the tears in her breast welling up for Ari-da. Only there, only in Ari-da's kind heart would there be room for all her humiliation, neglect, and the agony of unbearable daily jealousy.

TWELVE

'No tickets, no problems, we'll drive,' bellowed Bikram. 'But I don't understand why you've planned to travel at night.'

'That's when it's cool. We'll have to bear the intense heat at Ajanta and Ellora in any case. If we also have to travel all that way in the heat, any head except an idiot's will ache,' answered Aritra.

Neelam had been sitting quietly for a long time. Esha was in the kitchen. The aroma of chicken in the pot. Seema and Aritra were absorbed in their argument with Bikram. Ari wanted Bikram to try getting tickets, or else hire a Land Rover. Bikram insisted on following the bus in his own car. Neelam felt as though she was visiting someone else's house. Someone she knew only slightly. The stiffness had not been dispelled. She was unable to match her enthusiasm to theirs. She was surrounded by an arc of extreme loneliness. There would soon be a time when no one would be able to enter this magic circle, and she would not be able to escape it either. She felt choked.

Pupu parked her scooter and came up then. She had been to a friend's place early in the morning. 'You're here, Bikram Kaku?' she said. 'You're very late. Kakima! Why didn't you come earlier? Have you met Mashi?'

Bikram reached out and grabbed her. A big smile on his face. Seema said, 'Have you grown taller again?'

'I look taller every time you see me. If I keep growing at this rate you won't need a flag staff anymore. You can fix the flag to my ear on Republic Day. What were you discussing, all of you?'

Aritra said, 'We're going to Aurangabad tomorrow night, Pup. You and your mother are staying back. You'll be all right, won't you? Such a bad time for your exams.'

'Why isn't Ma going?' asked Pupu. 'Is it because of me?'

'Naturally,' said Aritra.

'Absolutely no need. I can stay at the hostel with Prita for a few days. Why should Ma be stuck here? I wish I could go too. Such a fantastic group to travel with.'

'Your mother won't agree to leaving you behind, take it from me,' said Aritra.

Neelam said in a subdued voice, 'It won't be easy staying in the hostel and taking your exams, Pupu.'

'It's most convenient in the hostel, Ma. I'm going to miss Ajanta anyway, but if you miss it too . . . and Esha Mashi doesn't visit us every day.'

'But we haven't got a ticket for your mother.'

'Hardly matters,' said Bikram. 'What's the use of a big car that remains empty?'

Pupu said, 'You and Kakima are going too, aren't you, Bikram Kaku? I'm sure you'll be singing on the way. What has Dr Roy decided, Baba? Is he going with you?'

'He is.'

'How I wish my exam could be deferred.'

'Would you have enjoyed travelling with old people like us?' asked Aritra.

'Who's old? You people? A most interesting lot. Esha Mashi, Dr Roy, oooh! Bikram singing, Seema singing, think of me when you sing, Seema.'

Something had got into Neelam's eyes. They were watering. 'Splash water in your eyes, Neelam-di,' said Seema. 'Don't rub them.' Neelam left the room. Aritra was not at all keen on Neelam's going.

Mahanam, Seema and Bikram left around noon after lunch at Neelam's house. The bus would leave at night. Neelam would travel on Mahanam's ticket. Bikram had suggested that Seema, Esha and Neelam should all go in his car. There was plenty of space, it didn't matter if one of the tickets was wasted. No problem. Arita said, 'Yes, three women with you, you will show off and drive the car off a cliff.' Bikram and the rest would wait one night for them. The next day they would go to Ellora together.

Neelam discovered that after the long uphill and downhill journey, they had finally arrived at the plains stretching to the horizon. The sun was rising over Aurangabad. Fallow land as well as farms lay on both sides of the road. Aritra on one side of her and Esha on the other were both sunk in deep sleep. Neelam had kept herself awake all night. Softly she called, 'Wake up, Esha. We've reached Aurangabad, Ari.' Neelam felt as though Pupu had been standing by her side all night, holding a flaming torch. What a nightmarish journey!

They had planned to bathe at the rest house and then leave for Ellora. On the way they would pass the Daulatabad fort. The Maharashtra Tourism bus would leave around eight-thirty. When they got off the bus they found Bikram, Seema and Mahanam ready and waiting. Bikram said, 'We'll all go in the car behind the bus. I've worked it out with the guide.'

'That's best,' said Neelam. 'It's difficult to get into and out of a high bus all the time.'

It was a tight squeeze. Mahanam had occupied a lion's share of the space on the front seat, barely leaving room for Bikram's elbows. Aritra's leanness was trying to compensate for it. Whatever space Seema and Esha had left on the back seat had been utilized by Neelam. 'It's quite comfortable,' said Neelam happily. Aritra said, 'Make sure your comfort doesn't mean discomfort for others,' said Aritra. 'Not to worry, Bhabi,' said Bikram. 'Why don't you lean back, Esha-di, I'll shift forward.' Mahanam said, 'You should exercise, Neelam, if only out of consideration for others.' Neelam said, 'I can't bear all this criticism anymore.' Esha was silent. She and Piku had a pact—whenever either of them travelled anywhere, they always wrote to the other one with every last detail. Esha hadn't written to Piku yet. She was wondering whether to write tonight.

The interiors of the car smelt of middle-age desire. It was redolent in the air. Had a young girl like Pupu been here, the tender scent of her personality would have permeated everything. Everyone—at least, most of them—could indistinctly sense a powerful sexual whirlwind willing itself within them. Aritra felt a strong desire for Esha. Seema wanted her husband, whom she had never had in the fullest sense. Bikram wanted Esha if possible, or else Neelam, or else any other woman except Seema, whom he was habituated to. Neelam wanted Mahanam. Mahanam did not want anyone in particular, but a desire for desire was taking shape silently, swamping his very existence. Sensing its presence within a mist of consciousness, he was stricken by the possibility of a bond in the near future and yet, the longing in his body and mind were a natural outcome of the demands of his soul. Understanding this wish and its possible form of fulfilment was building a quiet expectation. Esha wanted Ajanta, complete with all its nuanced shades of historical, mythical, artistic and human form and colour. This wanting was so deep that she was oblivious to the scent of sex in the atmosphere. Neelam was seated on one side of her, Seema on the other. No one seemed to perceive her silent, almost concealed presence between them. She too was not aware of anyone else. She always turned deeply self-absorbed when she was confronted with an extreme situation. She didn't want to talk, her tongue seemed to go to sleep, her throat was sunk in a dream. Her limbs grew heavy. It needed great effort to be able to move again.

The walls of Daulatabad fort began a long way away from the citadel. Nothing behind them was visible. Only the dilapidated wall kept flowing endlessly. The bus had stopped. Armed with sunglasses, umbrellas, flasks and camera, the tourists had got off. After Bikram had parked,

Esha stood by herself at a distance. She did not want to enter. The others were walking on ahead. Why waste time on a historical object like this fort, whose testimony you had already taken, which would offer you nothing by way of capital for living? How do you know it won't? Instinct. You could be wrong. Intuition doesn't make a mistake all of a sudden. Bringing this little debate with herself to a close, Esha remained outside the fort. There was a shop beneath a makeshift roof, with a few scattered wooden benches. For the first time on this journey, Esha asked for a glass of Maharashtra's famous sugarcane juice, not so much out of thirst as out of the need to pass the time. People stared if you sat idly. She would have to ask for another glass if necessary.

Esha had been prepared to sit by herself for a long time. However, she saw a few members of her group returning. Not together, but each at their own pace.

Bikram was the first to arrive. Settling his bulk on a plank of wood, he began to sing a ghazal. Bikram had been introduced to Esha, but they had not become acquainted. What little he had seen had stoked his curiosity enormously. Containing it was a precondition of civility, but Bikram cared nothing for it. The slightest encouragement from Esha would have led him to express his naked inquisitiveness, but Esha was not encouraging him. She wasn't ignoring or rebuffing him either, realized Bikram, so he wasn't angry. The fact was that, like the alligator that knows nothing of fragrant flowers or the Great Bear, Bikram knew nothing of Esha. And yet, because externally they belonged to the same human species, he considered knowing her part of his natural rights.

Bikram was followed by Aritra. He could be seen returning before Bikram was even halfway through his song. His brows were creased. Sounding annoyed, he said, 'Just dust everywhere. Rubbish. Not every stone is hungry enough to talk.'

'You're underestimating the fort, Dada,' said Bikram. 'There are several defence mechanisms in there. At some places footsteps echo in secret chambers at the top, elsewhere two open blades descend to decapitate intruders. The guide even demonstrates some of these in thrilling ways. In the darkness he takes away matches and torches from everyone, then announces dramatically that he's about to show them something spectacular. When the crowd surges forward, he says, don't move, anyone. Then he lights a single matchstick and a pit is revealed, so deep that its bottom cannot be seen.'

'Really?' said Esha. 'I'm scared just to think of it. Is it safe in there? The other three are still inside.'

'They'll be fine,' said Bikram. 'Chowdhury-da here could have fallen though, he's both restless and reckless.' Holding his palm up in assurance, he said, 'No Esha-ji, no one can fall in, the pit is fenced off.'

'You've seen it before, then?'

'Of course. That's why I didn't go inside. Have you any idea how many steps one has to climb? People used to go up on horseback—once is enough.'

'Have you been too, Ari?'

'No,' said Ari grimly.

'Why didn't you, then? It seems interesting.'

'Why didn't you, for that matter?'

Bikram practically rolled with laughter. 'See, Esha-ji, since you didn't go, Chowdhury-da didn't either.'

Esha only said, 'I'm preserving my energy for Ellora and Ajanta.'

Neelam was seen returning a little later, her face red with exertion. Flopping down in the shade of the tree, she said, 'Uff! This isn't for me.'

Seema did not return because she was sure that Neelam and Esha would guard each other. She followed Mahanam up the steps as he went forward with unruffled but indomitable curiosity. He had to find out where it was leading him. And so, when they reached Ellora, he followed the official guide slowly past the Buddhist caves, the Jain caves, and the multistoried viharas and arrived at the courtyard of the Kailash temple, where he observed his companions looking closely at what Ellora had to offer, while the official party of tourists lagged behind, for the guide was delivering detailed lectures at the entrances to several of the caves. Since the group included two young Japanese men, the guide had to resort to broken Japanese from time to time. Mahanam brought his notebook out. Bikram and Aritra were taking photographs.

Esha said, 'I'm going to take just a few pictures, Mahanam-da. Please guide me.'

Mahanam said, 'Just follow me. I'm not going to take too many either.'

Neelam was finding it difficult to climb on to the high terrace. Slinging his camera round his neck, Bikram ran up to her, picking her up in his arms and depositing her on the terrace. Holding his hand out to Esha, he said, 'I can use my other arm to pick you up too.' Seema was skipping up the steps lightly. 'How many times can Sita cross the Lakshman rekha and submit herself to Ravana?' she said. Aritra shouted in Mahanam's direction, 'Don't go so far ahead, Mahanam-da. The guide is out of sight, who will show us around if you're not here?'

Mahanam had indeed walked on ahead. He had understood Bikram's motives. The way Bikram had held Neelam in his arms to hoist her on the terrace had appeared distasteful to him. He stopped to let Aritra catch up. Appearing at the edge of the terrace, he said loudly, 'Look up, all of you. You'll see that the temple has been carved out of the hill. The hill is made of soft basalt. The architects had done their homework before starting on the temple. These temples or caves were not built upwards from the foundations, as is usually the case. The artists carved their way down the hillside. You can see the marks left by the chisels and hammers if you look upwards.'

Proceeding along the corridor on the left, he addressed Seema. 'Don't miss the relief sculptures depicting Shiva and Parvati playing dice. Parvati is rising to her feet with the support of her arm, which rests on the ground. A rustic pose. The artist has demonstrated how well he knows it. Here's the scene of their marriage. Look at Parvati's expression, Neelam, here too she takes the form of a bashful woman. Look at the Tripurantak Shiva, Bikram. Have you noticed, Ari, how different the imagination here is from the familiar Chola period figure of the Nataraj dancing symbolically within a ring of fire, or from the folk art figure of a pot-bellied Ashutosh? This Shiva is not four-armed. And much younger, too. These different versions of Shiva are probably the missing links in the history of the blending of Aryan and non-Aryan cultures. Like Mahishashurmardini, even in the time of war he has a reassuring smile on his face.'

'Shiva was actually a young man at the time,' said Bikram. 'Don't you see his slim waist? This was when Parvati or Durga fell in love with him. Later he became paunchy with age, and though she didn't divorce him, Parvati lost interest. That was it, Shiva turned into a mendicant. The beggar god. I roamed the village roads seeking alms.'

Seema said, 'Why are you bringing age into it? Many so-called young men also grow bellies. Especially considering how much the gods drank.'

'That's true,' said Mahanam. 'When the churning of the ocean created sura, or nectar, it was because they rejected it that asuras were named "asuras", while the gods were named "suras" because they accepted it. But there is debate over whether this nectar was liqueur, liquor, or wine. It is usually considered a symbol.'

Esha said, 'But it isn't impossible that an ancient Aryan race would consider alcohol a necessity of life. They came from very cold areas, after all. What if they expressed the folk memory of this addiction as myth?'

Aritra said, 'I think the myth of the churning of the oceans is a fertility myth. The sea is the vagina and Mandar hill is a symbol of the penis. Those who emerged—

Lakshmi, Urvashi, Apsara, Dhanwantari—are the results of this sexual act.'

Bikram had been listening open-mouthed. 'Bravo, Chowdhury-da, bravo!' he said. 'You've beaten even the latest American porn hollow.'

Mahanam asked in surprise, 'Did you read this somewhere, Aritra? Or is it your own conclusion?'

Aritra said, 'Someone else may have said it too. But I don't recall reading it. It occurred to me right now.'

Bikram was about to toss away the cigarette he'd been smoking. Seema grabbed his elbow from the back, saying, 'How can you pollute a temple?'

'Where should I get rid of this then?' asked Bikram irritably.

'Give it to me.' Seema stubbed it out on the handle of her umbrella, and then put it in a polythene packet which she took out of her bag.'

'How resourceful you are,' said Mahanam with a smile. 'Do you always have packets like that?'

'I have no choice,' said Seema. 'Given his habits, he could litter anywhere, who else but me will clean up after him?'

Mahanam exchanged glances of astonishment with Esha. 'Really Seemachalam, you are fantastic,' said Aritra.

They continued viewing the relief sculptures on the walls of the temple, eventually joining the other tourists. Carved in rock but delicate, frozen in stone forever but soaring. They had no wings like the angels in Christian images, and yet there could be no doubt from their postures that they were completely free of terrestrial gravity. The scientist's way of converting solid matter to energy leads to explosions that can destroy the world, but the artist's way results in explosions of pure joy. This flying, living stone had made humans feel lighter in their hearts for aeons.

The others had walked on ahead. Even after Esha had photographed the statue of the dancing Shiva, she remained standing before it. Bowing to it in her head. When she saw Bikram return, she started moving again. Almost like the figure of Nataraj.

When they came out of the Kailash temple, Neelam said, 'I have no wish to see the Jain caves. I'm going to sit in the car.'

The guide said, 'Come in December or January next time, Madam. Aurangabad is hot in any case because it is in the shadow of the monsoon, and moreover these regions are built on lava. The soil is not very deep here.'

They stood in the open expanse. Bikram and Aritra took group photographs. Esha said, 'You took so many pictures of architecture and sculptures, Mahanam-da, but not a single one of people. So human memories have no value for you?'

When Mahanam pointed his camera like an embarrassed, obedient adolescent, even Bikram started laughing. Hiding her face with her hands, Esha said, smiling, 'I won't let you photograph me.'

'Don't worry,' said Ari. 'All of you are in my photos. Neelam ran away, but I know a studio, you'll see how I can include her too.'

'Are you a very good photographer, Ari?' asked Mahanam. 'What camera do you use?'

'A very old Roliflex.'

'If some of my photographs don't turn out well, will you give me some prints of yours?'

'Of course,' said Aritra. 'I should give them anyway as fees for your services as a guide. To tell you the truth, Mahanam-da, it was this Kailash temple that appealed to me the most. Any idea why?'

Mahanam said, 'When art reaches a great height, it acquires a new dimension. The statue of Bahubali at Shravanabelagola or the chariot at Mahabalipuram made me realize this. We consider the sky and the earth, mountains and oceans, the creation of god—but all these sculptures and architectural works approach them in greatness.'

'Doesn't talent count?' said Esha. 'The expressions, postures, hand movement. The Mukteshwar temple in Orissa might be a plaything compared to Konark or Lingaraja, but it's exquisite.'

'Of course it counts. If the sky and the sea and the mountain are the backdrop, trees and creatures and fruits and flowers are the details. The Kailash temple is a manifestation of this enormous global backdrop, and all the carvings, sculptures and figures on its walls are the details.'

Esha said, 'Mahanam-da, all the art in the world, especially from the ancient world, are based on religion, and yet this same religion, the bearer of the magnificent, is now the most hostile to us.'

'Actually, Esha, religion too is another expression for our desire for find excesses in our lives. I believe the same inspiration is at work behind religion and behind art. Wonder, reverence, our humble submission to vastness—all of these found one form of expression in religion, and another in art. Naturally, the two merged. But with the passage of time, the more religion acquired the weaknesses of institutionalization and of narrow rituals, along with flawed principles, the more its gulf with art widened.'

Aritra said, 'The number of religions keeps multiplying too. The Hindu, Muslim, Christian, Buddhist or Sikh faiths are not enough anymore. Shakta, Shaiva, Vaishnav, Orthodox Greek, Church of England, Unitarian—hundreds of branches. Now there's a new faith named Ba'hai. Today's Iskcon doesn't seem to be the old Vaishnav sect either.'

'These things are not as much a part of religious studies as they are of sociology, Aritra,' said Mahanam. 'The sects you mention are mostly the result of reforms in existing religions. Christianity was born to reform Judaism. The Brahmo and Sikh faiths were both revolutions aimed at reforming Hinduism. I believe even the Ba'hai faith is an attempt to reform Islam.'

THIRTEEN

Esha went for a bath after finishing her letter to Piku. Four multiplied by two: eight pages. Piku must have been expecting a letter much earlier. But Esha had not been in touch since sending a telegram after her arrival in Pune. The phase of her life with which she had been reconnected in Pune had no relationship with Piku. My friend and his wife are taking very good care of me, I like their daughter very much—she could have written a non-committal letter to this effect, but Piku wouldn't have been satisfied. And yet, if she were to write, many other things would have crept in—how Priyalkarnagar had peeled layers of skin off her mind like an onion, the drama of unravelling the knots of memory, sadness, enjoyment and complexity, the joy and fear of being reunited with people she had known. Today's experience had been much more impersonal in comparison. So she had no hesitation writing tonight. During her bath she had realized that even fatigue could be enjoyable. She had paused to explore all the important places in Aurangabad—Bibi ka Maqbara, Aurangzeb's grave, everything—and collected scenes and information for Piku's benefit. Roasted in the sun, their hair unkempt, half a dozen humans returned to the rest house. Bikram and Seema had sung songs all evening, their energy was inexhaustible. Fatigue had wrapped her in its arms. A luxurious idleness.

Esha entered the room she was sharing with Seema and Neelam, filling it with the lovely fragrance of soap and talcum powder. In her pink nightdress Seema looked like a nylon doll lying on the bed and cleaning the cream off her face. Neelam lay on her stomach, letting the fan cool her back. Taking in the scene with a single glance, Esha began to comb her hair. Watching others rest made her own body feel restful.

Sitting up, Seema suddenly asked, 'Why didn't you get married, Esha-di?'

Braiding her hair, Esha said, 'Just didn't get round to it.'

Seema said, 'Women like you shouldn't stay unmarried.'

'But why?' smiled Esha. 'Do you want everyone's wings to be clipped because you've chosen to clip yours?'

'That's not it,' said Seema. 'How else will you protect yourself in a male-dominated world?'

'I'm doing it. Have been doing it all this while.'

'You know,' said Seema, 'when an attractive object is unclaimed people assume it's public property.'

Esha stopped smiling. 'Do you consider yourself an object, Seema? As property? Still?'

'Whether I do or not, Esha-di, it doesn't stop people from thinking that way.'

Esha said sadly, 'I cannot think of myself that way, so I don't think about what people think either. I'm mortified to know you do. Please Seema, don't think of yourself or me as an object.'

'What choice do I have?' said Seema. 'That's what the men in our society think. Perhaps because they have to take the responsibility for protecting us.'

'Maybe men don't think that way, Seema, maybe we force them. You shouldn't be too dependent on anyone. The police and the military for instance are there to protect us. Does that mean they should consider people objects or their own property? Society will always have a division of labour, according to each one's strengths. Why not prepare yourself in a way that lets some people depend on you too?'

'The person who's supposed to depend on me, Tito, is learning to depend on other people in Dehradun, Esha-di. And Tito's father? He is completely independent.'

'If Tito's father is independent, you should be, too. By not depending on you he's ensuring you're not a prisoner. What's coming in the way of your independence, then?'

Seema began to laugh. 'You don't know, Esha-di, some people's independence comes from the dependence of others.'

Esha said, 'No Seema, I've noticed that women feel a certain glory in considering themselves beholden to their husbands or to other men. "Let me ask him, he doesn't want to, he was saying . . ." you will often hear such statements from women who are well-educated, possibly financially independent too. I don't know if this is a psychological explanation, but I think you too feel proud to think of yourself as your husband's property, you consider yourself far superior to independent women like me, isn't that so?'

'Are you angry with me, Esha-di?'

Neelam had been listening quietly all this while. Now she said, 'Expressions like "unclaimed" or "public property" are not at all respectful, Seema. I don't know why you used them.'

Esha intervened quickly, 'That's not exactly what Seema meant, Neelam, I understand the points she's making. I'm not angry, merely a little worked up. But my experience shows that women are very complex characters. They don't know what they want. They're caught up in doubts about everything. Wanting and not wanting at the same time. I don't know why this is so.'

Neelam sat up. 'You're absolutely right, Esha. Wanting and not wanting at the same time. Why? Why are we so bizarre?'

Seema said, 'So you too suffer from wanting and not wanting at the same time, Esha-di? What if this is a general characteristic of all women?'

'No Seema, I don't suffer from it,' said Esha. 'Perhaps I'm not entirely a woman in that case. When I want something it's never by mistake. If there's a valid reason, such as this tremendous urge to visit Ajanta and Ellora, I do whatever possible to make it happen. And I certainly do not feel afterwards that I didn't want to, that I was wrong. But I suffer from a different illness, though you have to think about whether to call it an illness or not, which is to have something and yet not have it at the same time.'

'What on earth is that?' asked Seema curiously.

'You're a child, you won't understand,' Neelam told her.

Seema said in a small voice, 'No Neelam-di, my son is thirteen, I've been married fifteen years. I understand very well what it is to have and yet not have something. I understand mine. I was only trying to understand what it means for others, for Esha-di, for you.'

The chirping of crickets had begun. The bright light in the lawn was switched off, leaving only a dim glow. Night meant peace. Daylight never seemed to wane here. The sleeping buses were visible at a distance through the window. They would stretch and start moving again tomorrow morning. How deep their repose was. But every time Aritra closed his eyes he could see ugly scenes. Only if he was secure about Neelam could he turn his attention fully to Esha. But Neelam wasn't offering him that certainty. She had summoned Bikram, and Mahanam had floated up from some distant past. She had informed Mahanam that she was the mother of his child. Mahanam hadn't even known. She had invited him home and given him lunch. And it was primarily she who had brought him on this trip. Mahanam would have come anyway, but getting him to accompany Aritra and Esha was a tactical move on Neelam's part. Aritra Chowdhury was about to be checkmated by a pawn. Bikram Seal was blocking his way on one side, and Mahanam Roy on the other. Neelam herself was positioned in a third direction, holding the scales of blindfolded justice in to weigh his achievements and failures. But a river long forgotten had roared back into his bloodstream. Esha was like the legendary magnet in the Sun Temple at Konark. And Aritra, a Portuguese ship. Even if he could not arrive in one piece, all the iron in his body would be shattered and deposited on Esha's shore.

Mahanam was performing the shavasana with his eyes closed, lying flat on his back. He was in the habit of exercising every evening, but he hadn't been up to it today because of the exertion. The evening session of music had been a pleasant one. Every time he tried to unknot his legs and sink into detachment through his shavasana, what appeared before his eyes indistinctly was the figure of the goddess Kali sitting on a corpse. What a strange delusion. What he had seen today was Parvati as Gauri, but this fresh memory had easily been supplanted by another image—was this some Tantric tradition flowing in his blood? The pervasive darkness of the figure gradually occupied his mental world. He felt overcome by a wondrous drowsiness. If this rhythm grew more insistent, what would Mahanam fill the pages of his book with? He began to fight it with all the power at his disposal. He would have to keep the force of his conscience alive. He did not wish to drown himself now in the pleasures of emptiness and blackness. Little by little, his willpower took him to the land of conscious slumber. Mahanam sighed deeply.

Suddenly he heard a faint sound. Mahanam went from willed sleep to willed wakefulness. He saw the door closing slowly. Startled, he realized that both the other beds were empty. Neither of his two companions was in the room. There was plenty of money in here. An unknown land. Dead of night. Mahanam sat up in his bed. Let the door remain shut, but he would stay awake till they returned and locked the door. There were two large windows on the left.

Suddenly Mahanam saw Bikram walking across the lawn in the dim light. And, following him at a distance, Aritra. Were they strolling outside because they couldn't sleep? At this hour of the night! In the ghostly glow on the lawn they looked like wild animals, Bikram for his enormous, outsized form and Aritra for his wary, catlike movements. Mahanam was surprised to see Bikram step off the path and walk towards their rooms. The three women were in the next room, he was standing next to its large window, at first glance the garden looked like a jungle with a gorilla-like humanoid creature in it. Going up to the window, Mahanam cleared his throat, whereupon Bikram whirled round and found himself face to face with Aritra.

'What are you doing?' said Aritra in a muffled, angry voice.

'What are YOU doing?' Bikram countered belligerently.

'You want to know? Waiting to nab you red-handed.'

'Have I stolen something?'

'Do it if you dare.'

'Careful, Chowdhury-da. There's a limit to insults, I won't tolerate it, there will be violence.'

Mahanam was amused. Everyone wanted to fight a duel with Aritra. Aritra had been born a valorous man. Always at loggerheads with other men. There was no way to settle things except through frontal combat. Who knew what kind of man this Bikram Seal was. If Aritra was mythical, Bikram was prehistoric.

'What's the matter, Aritra, Bikram?' he asked from the window.

Both of them turned towards him in surprise. Possibly

someone had appeared at the window of the next room too. There was a faint sound of the shutters being closed. Aritra strode away. Bikram went in the opposite direction. Aritra entered the room, Mahanam was back in bed, he could hear Aritra's agitated breathing. Aritra was saying in a low voice, 'Bastard, scoundrel!' Bikram entered about ten minutes later, locking the door loudly. His bed creaked. Within five minutes Mahanam could hear him snoring.

When the women got ready in the morning and gathered in the dining room, Aritra said, 'We're taking the bus today. I've booked four seats. It's too much of a squeeze in the car.'

'No problem,' said Bikram.

'Oh no,' said Seema, 'I'll have to go alone with you in the car.'

'You can take the bus too, who's stopping you? I love driving by myself.'

'Yes, and while I take the bus, you'll have an accident,' said Seema.

'How many cars on this road to have a collision with? I might run into the tourism bus though. Just imagine how fast I can drive on these empty roads.' Bikram's expression revealed the animal pleasure of speed. He always found some form of pleasure or the other.

'Have you seen auto races?' said Seema. 'Some of the cars just turn upside down. Going up in flames. The burnt bodies of the drivers have to be pulled out. For this reason alone I'm travelling in your car today. And you will let me drive too.' Seema walked across the room to the other side as she spoke. 'I know why Ari-da booked seats on the bus.

What were you arguing about last night? Must you fight even on a holiday?'

Winking, Bikram said, 'I really wound him up last night. He was livid. As it is the man has a filthy mind.'

'Did you expect to just reach in through the window and pull one of us out like a rag doll?' asked Seema without smiling.

Bikram burst out laughing. 'Why would I have to pull anyone out? Wouldn't you have come if I'd asked you? Who wants to be alone on such a lovely, thrilling night?'

Seema said, 'Big mistake. Don't imagine I will come whenever you ask me to.'

Quickly lighting a cigarette to hide his discomfiture, Bikram said, 'All right, enough. Enough nonsense. Let's go now.'

Mahanam and Neelam were seated in the very first row. Aritra sat with Esha five rows behind them. The seats had high backs. Mahanam was unusually tall. Sometimes it is the length of their legs that leads to a difference in height. But Mahanam was also taller than most from the waist upwards. Which was why his light blue collar and a head full of wavy hair were visible from the back. Whenever he looked sideways, his nose, the flow of his eyes and the lines of his beard could be seen. Neelam was out of sight. But still Aritra was reassured today. Bikram wasn't next to her. The ugly sight of Bikram's picking Neelam up in his arms to deposit her on the terrace of the Kailash temple would not be repeated. Of course, he had had to leave the seat next to hers to Mahanam. But Mahanam wasn't Bikram. If sitting next to him brought some of Neelam's college romance back to her, so be it. Aritra had got a seat next to Esha's. Aritra was next to Esha. Aritra and Esha.

Aritra was looking at his favourite sight, Esha, in different ways—directly, from the corner of his eyes, turning towards her. A glittering necklace around her neck, a few wisps of hair, curled and small, behind her hair. Her blue sari was reflected on her forehead. Esha was looking darker than usual. The sun had been overhead most of the previous day. How his heart, his joy, brimmed over at the sight of this dark complexion. The bus was redolent with its glow, Aritra's mind too.

'What trees are those, Ari, do you know?' asked Esha. 'There were many of them outside the Daulatabad fort too.'

'Which trees? Oh those! Those are silkcotton trees. Semul.'

'They have such shiny silvery bark. Just look at them in the sunlight. Like silver trees. Standing there with their branches. No flowers or anything. So beautiful. See how many there are. They're like trees of light. Gardens of heaven.'

'Didn't you know silk is cultivated in Maharashtra? How strange.'

'Oh, is this where it comes from? Imagine the black soil giving birth to light. Do you know, Ari, from the train I saw a herd of rock elephants in the bed of a dry river. If only I could have shown you. Straight out of the Jatakas. Small, medium, large, elephants in all sizes.'

'You wanted to show me, Esha? Tell me truly, me?'

'I wanted to show someone. The joy of seeing something

beautiful isn't complete unless it's shared.'

'You're very cruel, Esha. Couldn't you have lied and said it was only me you wanted to show it to?'

'But wouldn't you have felt bad if you knew I was lying?' Esha smiled at him. How much more cruel would he consider her if she told him that she had had no specific feeling about him till meeting him at Kalyan?

'Esha, tell me you've come to me, to see me, to be seen by me, to be close to me—say it once, at least once.'

Esha said, 'Honestly Ari, I'm here to visit Ajanta, I cannot explain how strongly it's been calling me for some time now. My prayer to life is that I get to see the Sistine Chapel.'

A miserable Aritra said, 'But still you won't say it. Not even as a lie. Can the attraction of Ajanta be greater than a person's?'

Esha said, 'You said poets never die entirely, Ari. If, being a poet, you do not understand the attraction of Ajanta, whom will I explain it to?'

Taking Esha's hand in his and holding it tightly, Ari said, 'Don't tell me charming lies then, or secret truths. Doesn't the fact that I came to your mind in the context of Ajanta prove something?'

'What does it prove?' Esha smiled.

'It proves that:

I want, it's you alone I want still
A choking whisper in desolation's ear
In your absence I cannot bear
My presence, my future's dark and closed

Your name spells the meaning of eternal loss
Your name . . . just your name . . . just your name

Esha said, 'I'd never have come if I hadn't completely stopped wanting you. I wouldn't have been able to. If I'd still wanted you, the humiliation, the rejection, the agony of being used, would all have hurt like fresh, gaping wounds. All this has died a natural death. I can see you entirely impersonally now.'

Every word of Esha's was a knife being twisted in Aritra's heart. He said, 'How shall I seek your pardon, Esha, Presha? How? Forgive me, Esha.'

'How strange, Aritra. I did that a long time ago. Didn't I tell you that all these things have been turned to ashes and dispersed in the skies? It is because I have overcome those terrible shocks that I am who I am today. The ashes of those memories fell on the soil of my mind and made it fertile. I am happy that they took place and that they ended. And I can now seek your help to visit Ajanta along with Neelam. Ari, I . . . I'm hungry for experiences, parched, sometimes I wish I had a hundred bodies, a hundred minds . . .'

'And if you did? Would you not give one of them to me?'

'Life has to be drunk till the cup is drained, Ari, it needs so much time. So many minds. I think several lifetimes can pass having the same experience in different ways. Nothing's left over, there's always a shortage.'

'How could you be so cruel, Esha? You're not willing to give me even one of the hundreds of lifetimes, the hundreds of births. Maybe I did make a mistake, maybe I WAS unjust to you once. But still.'

'You didn't make a mistake, Ari. You were unjust, that's true. But it's not very serious in the context of one's entire life. You didn't do any permanent damage to me. On the contrary, your choice was right. Neelam is the one who has transformed you from your Bohemian existence to an ideal, successful, husband and father. She is your appropriate partner.'

'I've changed externally. Yes, I live comfortably. But can such homebound comfort be a man's ultimate objective? Esha, you could have been my inspiration, the one who would have helped me find my true north.'

Smiling, Esha said, 'Don't mind what I'm about to tell you, Ari. Humanity won't suffer if a few poems remain unwritten, but the larger the number of peaceful, beautiful and successful units of parents and children there are, the better it is for society. And besides, you left me because you wanted Neelam, having got Neelam now you want me, if you get me you'll definitely want someone else. This is your nature, more or less.'

'Very well, if getting you releases me from my evil planet, you will also find some sort of release, won't you? Although you haven't analysed me correctly at all, I'm saying this from your point of view.'

'Why do you keep making the same mistake, Ari? And besides, one of your notions is completely incorrect. You think Neelam is only a homemaker, a housewife, who can offer nothing by way of what you call inspiration, but you're wrong. The truth is that you haven't got Neelam entirely. And you don't even know this.'

'You're saying Mahanam is still in her heart . . .'

'No.' Esha laughed. 'Honestly Ari, I'm not saying anything of the sort, working in a commercial firm has really coarsened you. I cannot find a trace of Trilokesh Gaurav in you anymore.'

Neelam said, 'You take the window seat now, Mahanam-da. You're here to see the sights.'

'Haven't you come to see them too?'

'I have, but not the scenery.'

'Why have you vowed to see art but not nature?'

'There are things on this trip much more worthy of my curiosity than the scenery,' said Neelam brightly.

'Such as?'

'You, Esha, Ari.'

'Are you studying us? Aren't Seema and Bikram included? They too are worth seeing and listening to.'

'I'm done with seeing them, listening to them. You can.'

'No you're not done, Neelam. Like everyone else, they too are evolving constantly. If you're interested in variety, you cannot ignore them.'

'You haven't demanded an explanation from me, Mahanam-da,' Neelam said in a disappointed voice.

How could Mahanam tell her:

I never built on your body
A sky-kissing stairway to heaven
I never forgot you're a magic moment's gift

He said, 'Very well, explain. I'm putting you in the dock.'

Neelam was hurt. 'Your eyes are shining with laughter. Is this any way to demand an explanation?'

'Then I shan't ask for one,' said Mahanam. '"Does anyone want to excavate his heart for pain?"'

'No heart. No pain either. Nothing. There never was.'

'Don't say that. You don't have to be so poetic.' Mahanam laughed loudly.

'Is Neelam telling jokes?' said Aritra from the back.

'Great sense of humour,' said Mahanam, getting to his feet.

'She has a huge stock, Mahanam-da,' said Ari. 'I'm not sure whether all of them are suitable for you though.'

Neelam heaved with laughter when Mahanam sat down. Pleased, he said, 'It seems Ari has made you happy. That's why I'm not going to scold you. I hope you understand that. The most important thing is to be happy.'

'What makes you think I am? Because I've grown fat?'

Mahanam laughed loudly again.

Esha said, 'Neelam is having such a good time. Mahanam-da is enjoying himself so much. And you're whispering all kinds of morbid things in my ear. Be easy, Ari. Accept the truth simply.'

'If only the truth were simple. Truth has appeared to me in very complex form.'

'Don't laugh, Mahanam-da,' said Neelam. 'Obesity could be a sign of unhappiness too. It's nothing to laugh about.'

'Unhappy? Are you unhappy?'

'We're talking of illness. Disease. Not unhappiness.'

'What's wrong with you?'

'Might be dropsy.'

'Impossible. No one can travel or do household work with dropsy.'

'Could be a glandular problem.'

'It could. You're a doctor's daughter, I'm a doctor's nephew, let me see if I can diagnose the problem. Is it a thyroid problem? Your eyes don't suggest it is. Don't talk rubbish. You've just eaten yourself to this state. Do you have a drink or two at parties?'

'You think a drink or two can do this?' Neelam began to laugh. Mahanam didn't see the tears lurking behind the laughter.

The bus had stopped. The passengers got out to stretch their legs. Bikram came up to them with two glasses of sugarcane juice. Handing them to Neelam and Esha, he came back at lightning speed with two more glasses. Giving one to Mahanam, he offered the other one to Aritra in the manner of the Air India maharaja, saying, 'Here you are Dada.'

'Pour it over your own head,' snarled Aritra.

Bikram said, 'I thought you had to pour cold water on someone's head. Mistaken metaphor, Dada? That's the problem with anger. Flouts all rules. You know, don't you?'

Taking the glass from him, Seema went up to Aritra with a smile. 'Ari-da, please.'

'I'm smoking, Seemachal,' said Aritra with a smile.

'You can smoke anytime. You can't have sugarcane juice anytime.'

'All right then,' said Aritra, holding his hand out.

Bikram recited loudly, with suitable gestures:

What sorcery is this, friend, what magic do you know
No one can slay a helpless damsel just the way you do

Neelam, Esha and even Mahanam couldn't help but laugh.

FOURTEEN

The steps were cut into the hillside. The rest house was directly opposite. A quiet place. The guide said, 'You have a little time to look around on your own, please gather here in exactly ten minutes.' Ellora had no connection with human habitation, it was distant, not destroyed but abandoned. As though the relationship between its greatness and spiritual values was so deep that it avoided proximity. Ajanta seemed to have come a little closer to human civilization. And humans too had been emboldened to construct a place for rest nearby.

The guide said, 'In 1817, while hunting here on Ajanta hill, an English soldier spotted rows of arches and pillars on the side of a hill across the river. The Tapti basin lies on the other side of the mountain range, while the Deccan plateau is situated this side. The tiny Waghur river flows here through gaps in the mountains, curving like a horseshoe near the Saatkund falls. This is where the Ajanta caves are situated. There are thirty caves in all. Five of them are chaityas or meditation centres. The remaining twenty-five are all sangharams or viharas. Temples. The tenth cave is the main one. Ajanta was built slowly over the period between 200 BC and 400 AD. Then, with gaps of a few years now and then, the work continued till the seventh century. In other words, it represents almost seven hundred years of work.'

Seema was counting the steps as she climbed. 'Exactly one hundred, Esha-di,' she said. The higher they ascended the more did JPJ, Priyalkarnagar and Neelam recede from Aritra's mind, while the College Street crossing, Hazra Road, Cornwallis Street, Ashutosh Building and Esha came closer.

Entering the first cave temple, Esha said, 'This must be the last cave built, isn't it, Mahanam-da? It was carved out during the reign of the Chalukya kings, I'm told.'

She fell silent on walking deeper into the cave. How could this oblong cave with smooth walls, like a gigantic hall, have been carved out of the mountain? What extraordinary architecture. The Kailash temple was huge, regal. But for some reason this cave appeared even more astounding. So cool that it seemed to be air-conditioned.

The guide shone his torch to show the figures of Buddha in the interiors of the temple. Buddha was seated in the lotus position, as in Sarnath. The expression changed depending on the angle of the illumination. From one side he appeared to be smiling, from another, melancholy. And from the front, the Light of Asia was rapt in meditation.

Mahanam said, 'I don't know whether the artist meant to bring about this variety in his expressions. If he did, we have to say he was brilliant. But we are invariably reminded of the expressions of the three figures of the sun at Konark. Newly-risen, noonday, and sad and weary at sunset—do you remember, Aritra?'

Aritra said absently, 'No. The Konark figures of the sun are in Delhi.'

'That's the statue from the interior of the temple,' said Esha. 'Don't you remember the figures in blue stone outside?'

Mahanam said, 'The sculptor must have felt that that prince who had renounced his home because of the pain of his fellow humans could never have forgotten the agony. Perhaps the artist in him could not accept the detached sage, indifferent to both joys and sorrows. So these expressions of happiness and sadness had automatically emerged alongside spiritual peace from the hands of this talented sculptor.'

On Mahanam's request the guide now held his light up to the depiction of Avalokiteshwar Padmapani. Here the Bodhisattva held a bloomed lotus in his right hand, with a bejewelled crown on his head, diamond ear rings, and a necklace of one hundred pearls round his neck. The artists of Ajanta were particularly adept at painting pearls. Avalokiteshwar was standing in the well-known Tribhanga posture, immersed in his thoughts. Opposite this painting was the one of the Avalokiteshwar Bajrapani. The human world was infested with decay, death and disease. How could the Bodhisattva devote himself selfishly to private worship? Negating the lustre of ornaments and attire, of luxury and lavishness, the rapt, meditative compassion of Avalokiteshwar shone through.

The colours of the photographs in the Unesco albums were too loud. The actual colours were much more mature, subdued.

'So much better than the prints, aren't they, Esha-di?' said Seema.

'That's just what I was thinking.'

In the tiny chamber deeper within the cave, a huge panel showed Buddha rapt in meditation and the attack of the lord of death Mara. Accompanied, obviously, by soldiers. Mara's three daughters were present too.

Mahanam said, 'They've come to disrupt his meditation, but they might end up joining it themselves.'

'Siddhartha's power is so much stronger in comparison that Mara's daughters have also fallen under its spell,' said Esha. 'They're defeated in the sense that they are overwhelmed.'

Bikram said, 'These paintings are not lifelike at all. The bodies are bent and twisted in ways that are not even possible while dancing. Did they all learn Odissi?'

'Art is never lifelike,' said Aritra. 'Look at the full figures, they're completely neglected waist downwards.'

Moving further ahead, Bikram said, 'Oh, this is paradise! Indra's court in Amravati! When the fortunate go to heaven, this is how the nymphs make them sit on thrones and entertain them. How nice! To ensure that people do good deeds out of their greed to go to heaven, the disciples of Buddha went to so much trouble to carve out caves and make all these paintings.' Winking at Aritra, Bikram said, 'What do you think, Chowdhury-da, should you and I start earning some piety?'

The guide said, 'This is a tale from the Jatakas. The Mahajanak Jataka. The Bodhisattva was born as King Mahajanak. Here he is announcing his decision to abdicate and renounce the world, which is why Queen Sibali looks so dejected. The singing and dancing have stopped. The ladies of the palace are engaged in consultation and speculation.'

'Good god,' exclaimed Bikram.

Esha stopped in front of the image of Princess Krishna. She was the one whom Esha had dreamt of. Thrice in succession. After seeing the pictures in the Unesco album. Dark-skinned. Downcast eyes. How had the Buddhist artist learnt of such depths of despair? The melancholy of Avalokiteshwar was not the same as this suffering. 'Look, Ari, how miraculous this grief is. It pervades the entire cave.' Esha sounded desolate. 'They may look different—Sibali, Mara's daughters, Sumana, this princess—but they're the same in one way. Companionless. The finest men in the world have burdened a solitary woman with the sorrows of the entire world and renounced earthly life.'

Seema said, 'I'm telling you Esha-di, without one person's suffering another cannot achieve happiness. Are you saying this Princess Krishna is also Yashodhara?'

'Excellent idea, Seema,' said Esha. 'Could be. While Mara was under attack, and Siddhartha was acquiring his status of Buddha with great pomp and ceremony, perhaps an artist was reminded by this scene of the suffering of the queen in the joyless palace in Kapilavastu. It could also be the case Seema that the bereft, unhappy female character seen everywhere in all these tales from the Jataka and the Buddhacharita has been depicted symbolically. An open symbol of womanhood. You can analyse it as you like.'

Mahanam was standing behind them, listening. 'Don't you have something to add, Neelam?' he said.

Neelam's eyes were brimming with tears. 'What can I say, it seems to me that this is a hapless woman who has got so many things and yet got nothing, for whom getting everything has been negated, turned into a failure, by the one big thing she hasn't got.'

Smiling, Aritra said, 'Since I used to write poetry once upon a time, I had assumed I was the only poet in this group. That I was the only one who could understand the artists of Ajanta correctly. Now I see my notion was completely wrong. Not me, it is these three women here who are the real poets.'

Mahanam said thoughtfully, 'Three women of the twentieth century can see the truths of life in paintings from the seventh century. Can you gauge the immensity of this artist's success? What would he have done had he been here today?'

'I'm sure he would have exclaimed, "Wow!"' said Bikram.

FIFTEEN

Each of them reacted differently to their tour of Ajanta. No one had paid any attention to Bikram throughout. Not even Seema, who seemed to have gathered new strength and stood in Bikram's path like a challenge. Bikram hadn't realized this clearly. But he had experienced a certain discomfort with Seema from the time of their trip to Ellora and Ajanta. Seema seemed to have become someone, a positive person with a distinctive personality.

The dark-eyed, cry baby whom he had eloped with from her Chunchura home fifteen years ago, who had taken a lot out of him over these past fifteen years while he had tried to rid her of her pouting and weeping, whom he now considered little more important than the bronze figure in the landing of his house in Thane, that very same Seema was now reprimanding him with polished language and subtle gestures, without sounding as though she was nagging him. Seema was speaking. Esha had turned towards her with wonder in her eyes. Mahanam, Dr Mahanam Roy, was talking to her as an equal, as though she was a fellow-speaker at a conference. Aritra Chowdhury had placed his hand on Seema's shoulders delicately, as though they were fragile and valuable. Like the panels at Ajanta, a sequence of these images appeared before Bikram's eyes like a living fresco. He was not the painter, in fact he was not even being accorded any importance as a viewer. The images were actions and reactions to one another. Bikram's 500-watt eyes had no effect on them, they were illuminated by some other source of light. Bikram could not understand this fresco. While the figures on the Ajanta panels were virtually unclothed, the characters in this living fresco were covered with some fine transparent muslin over their regular clothes, which made the familiar appear half-familiar, and the half-familiar, completely unfamiliar. He could not recognize Seema clearly. Aritra Chowdhury was now a total stranger.

Only in one of the caves had Bikram had the opportunity for receiving public acknowledgement. The guide said, 'This cave was probably used as a lecture hall. Stand at the centre, one of you, and say or sing something. The rest of you will hear it as you would on loudspeakers, complete with the echo.'

'Why don't you go, Bikram-babu,' Esha said.

Bikram had forgotten his music these days. He remembered only a few favourites that he had sung many times. In a deliberate attempt to vent his anger, he started singing a self-composed parody:

'Poor woman, you lurk behind the sage as his partner
You dangle from the langur's hands like a grape

Why can't you be the sweet and sour pickle with my bread
Poor woman.'

The notes spread to every corner of the cave. How amazing this auditorium made by the Buddhists was. Bikram felt very self-satisfied under the impression that, after all these years, he had finally injected some life into a place where the sages must once have bored young apprentice monks with a stream of instructions. Seema said, 'I want to sing a song too, may I?' 'Of course,' said the guide. Seema took a position within the circle of attention of her audience, and sang a few lines from Rabindranath's 'Chandalika'.

Then, kneeling suddenly, she sang in a high voice and a different scale, '*Buddhang saranang gachhami, Sanghang saranang gachhami, Dhammang saranang gachhami.*' I turn to Buddha for sanctuary. I turn to the Sangha for sanctuary. I turn to Dhamma for sanctuary.

A tall, plump foreigner with an innocent face drew a cross on her breast, raising her blue eyes to the ceiling. The two Japanese young men knelt, joined their palms, and softly uttered a prayer in their own language. 'Would anyone else like to sing?' asked the guide. The first song that Bikram had sung had put him in the mood for a ghazal, but Seema had sprinkled holy water and dampened the atmosphere. Realizing that his singing wouldn't be received well, he walked out glumly.

The Buddhist workers had filled one cave after another with nude paintings. There was no doubt that these works of art were the result of suppressed libido from the succession of days spent in these caves without women for company after renunciating the world. As was the case with Khajuraho or Konark or the Jagannath temple. Their mentors, the Arhats, used to live in great happiness watching all these blue films, which Bikram had absolutely no objection to. But why not call a blue film a blue film! Who's protesting! If you dress it up in the garb of religious wisdom, though, that's another matter. Just like the alcohol-drinking tantrics and the bhairavi chakra of women and sexuality. But the images were not sufficiently arousing sexually. Unlike the sixty-four yoginis at Khajuraho, who made you break out in a sweat. These were dull, no spice, like Rabindra-Nritya in comparison to Kathak or Mohiniattam. Unless it was a hot mutton do-piyaza or murgh musallam, or at least beef kababs, Bikram couldn't savour it. And then half the colours had worn off, the plaster was peeling, why would anyone waste an entire day on all this unless they were absolutely mad?

The gigantic sculpture of Buddhadeva's Mahaparinirvana —his death, the release of the already released—had overwhelmed Neelam. A sal tree on either side, his disciples kneeling near his feet, the abandoned begging bowl in Ananda's hand. Kushinagar. The architecture had captivated her more than the paintings, the sculpture more than the architecture. The Neelam who had climbed up the hundred steps to the Ajanta hill was not the same one who had climbed down the same hundred steps. Someone addressed her from behind the chaityas in a sweet, sonorous voice: '*Samma-ditthi, samma-sankappa, samma-vaca, samma-kammanta, samma-ajiva, samma-vayama, samma-sati, samma-samadhi.*' The right view, right thinking, right speech, right action, right livelihood, right effort, right mindfulness, right concentration. Not once, but again and again.

Sarnath. Siddhartha seated with his hands in the Dharmachakra Mudra gesture. He had just attained the status of Buddha, and was saying, 'O five sages, comprehend the fundamental reason for the agony of our earthly ties. Longing and desire are the root causes. The longing for sensual pleasure, the desire for satisfying oneself. How can these be uprooted? Forsaking longing and desire without leaving a trace is the real way.'

Indeed, what have you done all your life besides travelling from one longing to another desire? How turbulent youth had been, how tumultuous. Enriched—or was it besmeared—by hundreds of hunting expeditions. It was terrifying now to even recall all those devoted, lusting expressions. Someone had watched over Neelam from concealment to ensure that her sexual indulgence did not take her too far on the road to perdition. He had done what he had to. Neelam began to pray ritually after this. Only, what was it but a prayer to desire? A demand for compensation—or a plea to get back what she had lost—was woven into her sacred offerings of flowers and fruit. This form of worship was not genuine. It was self-deception, cheating too. See what a devoted disciple I am, I don't even drink a glass of water before offering it to the gods. Having walked around the ten caves at Ajanta, Neelam had understood what worship really meant.

The devotion, offerings, chanting, resolve, meditation and self-sacrifice of a multitude of devotees had been frozen in stone by the lines and the flow of the works of art here. Their sharp intensity had remained alive for more than thirteen hundred years—*samma-ditthi, samma-sankappa, samma-vaca. Om namah, Buddha dibakaray, gotam chandimay, sakyanandanay, nama namah*.

Buddhadeva had given householders the right to be Buddhists too. They would follow the eightfold path. It wasn't important whether you were a Buddhist or not. It didn't make any difference whether you followed a specific religion or not. But with this gigantic sculpture of Buddha's Mahaparinirvana before her, would Neelam be returning to the same home? How constricted it was, how impure its décor. What a strong smell of desire pervaded every corner—cigarette packets, beer bottles, meat, onion, garlic, envy, suspicion, rage, adultery. How would the great one enter there? He might be able to shrink his body, but how would he minimize his soul? Neelam said in her head—you have done me a favour by visiting my house, Esha. The glittering curtain in front of my eyes has been lifted. This is what they mean when they say *hiranmayena patrena satyasyapihitam mukham*—My Lord, Sustainer of Lives, your dazzling effulgence covers your face. A veil of false lustre is drawn over our eyes. We see it whenever we look, we think we are happy. We live in a fool's paradise. The truth will not be visible till this veil falls. I give Aritra to you, Esha. One day I had snatched him from your hands. I had felt great pride, huge self-satisfaction, a tremendous sense of victory that the brightest object of women's desire in the College Street area had left you for me. How selfish that pride was. I can feel in my bones now how wrong it was, how childish. I am returning Aritra to you. I give Mahanam to you too. Once I had deceived, yes, deceived, Mahanam. He did not punish me, demanded no compensation. But if he wants, if he really wants, I'll give Pupu to him too. When I go back I will reveal the truth to Pupu. I will not increase the burden of my sin by hiding from her the identity of the great man whose child she is. Pupu is quite calm and mature, if I explain to her properly she will definitely take it well. And if she didn't, if she forsook Neelam out of hatred and hurt, Neelam would bear that too. Her heart would break but she would bear it. She had got so much in life without paying for it. Pay now, Neelam Joshi, pay with your own hands, and then you can reach out to what is valuable, what is priceless. Neelam had effectively transformed herself into Rati, Mara's daughter. She kept thinking of what Mahanam had said, 'They've come to disrupt his meditation, but they might end up joining it themselves.' If it was possible for Mara's daughter herself to begin the act of devotion, would it be absolutely impossible for Neelam Joshi Chowdhury to purify her entire life up to now?

Aritra was so sunk in his own thoughts that he had not remotely realized the change in Neelam's. All of Ajanta was imbued with Esha for him. Every beloved, every princess, every woman was Esha-Presha. Why had the artists painted these beautiful women all over the caves with such dark skins? They had insight, they were farsighted too. Mahanam had said, 'Sakas, Huns, Pathans,

Moghuls . . . many tribes and many invaders have been to India, but none of them succeeded in influencing or distorting our aesthetics the way the British did. It was only after the advent of the British that we began to consider fair skin, and only fair skin, as a characteristic of beauty. A fair skin excuses all flaws. We had a more subtle vision earlier. Look at all these women painted here, the fair-skinned among them are handmaidens, friends, unimportant figures. Shireen, the queen of Persia, is fair-skinned as a tribute to fact, but all the women famed for their beauty are brown-skinned, some are quite dark. None of the beautiful women whom the Buddhist workers saw everywhere was fair-skinned in the European sense, a reality which they did not ignore.'

But Aritra was thinking of something else. Thirteen hundred years after its creation, a work of art no longer belonged to the artist. Its value lay in its message to the viewer, who was not concerned with the reality of the artist's world. He felt that his eternal love had receded into the shadows because she had not got him. Hence her melancholic form. Through the cave paintings of Ajanta she had come to convey her pain to him subtly, very subtly. Every sorrowful dark-skinned woman he stood in front of made his heart twist with pain. 'Poor woman of the shadows,' he said in his head.

What had Esha thought the day she had seen him with Neelam, when she had realized how intimate their relationship was? How terrible the pain must have been—even thinking of it made Aritra feel his heart being pierced by needles. Oh, how could he have been so cruel? Even after that, Esha had proposed marriage, despite being a woman, and what had Ari done? What could it be called but rejection under the garb of artificial words. And then? Then the tender young girl of nineteen, who thought of herself as mature and wise, that same Esha-Presha, had disappeared. She had vanished into thin air like a bubble. Only a notebook of poems had remained. Could a book match up to a person? He was looking at the faded painting of the dying princess Janapadakalyani in the seventeenth cave. His heart crumpled in agony. He discovered Esha standing motionless in front of the painting. There were several characters in the frame, the messenger of defeat stood with a crown in his hand, Kalyani was in her female companions' arms, Esha was busy looking at every small detail. Aritra found Neelam standing at a distance, looking at Esha. He decided that if Esha wanted, he would ask Neelam for a divorce. He had ensured that there was plenty of property registered in her name. She should have no difficulties. His life was supposed to have been divided between Neelam and Esha. Neelam had got his best years. The rest would be Esha's. But Pupu? Would he lose her? No, he wouldn't lose anyone. Not even Neelam. All of them had reached an age where changing one's partner should no longer be considered a reason for upheaval in the pattern of life. Pupu had grown up. Things would have to be explained to her. Neelam would live with Pupu as she did now. The truth was that her relationship with Aritra was like one between friends now, between brother and sister. What could come in the way, then? But it would not be possible in Pune. He could not take public criticism at this age. He would seek a transfer to Bombay. It wouldn't be a problem. Neatly distributing the problems of his life and his own wishes, Aritra was now recovering mentally. The restlessness that had pursued him once gradually disappeared. He kept stealing glances at Esha. As dark-skinned as a young sal tree, graceful, but the cleft in her chin alone was enough to madden him. As he watched Esha, he was certain that this was what she wanted too, not expressing it only because Pupu and Neelam would be hurt. When two trains moving at the same speed towards different destinations come side by side, each one feels the other isn't moving. Aritra had no idea that Esha's destination was different, he assumed that she had stopped. By his side. That he could touch her just by reaching out.

Seema was in a trance. Getting out of one's familiar environment often creates a sense of release. Especially since Seema was here with people whom she had not had the opportunity to be close to or travel with. Bikram's circle was limited to businessmen and brokers. He did not even belong to the world of music anymore. Wandering around with Esha and Mahanam, she had experienced the taste of freedom. As though their company had protected her from her horrible fate for a few days without interfering with her nature or shielding her in any way. Seema was discovering herself at every moment, and she was putting her discoveries to use. She had not realized that she still remembered the songs of 'Chandalika', which Bikram had taught her when she was young. When she saw the famous painting of Buddha, Yashodhara and Rahul in the seventeenth cave, her heart wanted to sing, 'Water, give me water.' She wanted to sing full-throated, 'I am parched with the heat, give me water.' As a matter of fact, Bikram had sung this very song, playing Ananda, in a performance he had directed himself at Rabindra Bhavan near Seema's childhood home. As Nature, Seema had sung with all her heart, 'My well is now the shoreless sea.' Now the same song wanted to rise like a fountain from her throat. She had even hummed a few lines. But it wasn't the yellowish figure of Buddha to whom her plea was directed. The object of her song was Bikram, Bikram and Bikram alone. For this man she was willing to be Mayabini, Dakini, Yogini, Bhogini, Rogini and even Sanyasini—she was ready to play sorceress, Tantric goddesses, woman of earthly pleasures, patient and even monk. Placing Bikram where Buddhadeva was, she was overcome by a secret, flowing emotion. Not once did she feel that superimposing Bikram on Buddha or Buddha on Bikram could be a gross error. Not a single pillar of logic stood on her terrain of passion. The rules of common sense did not apply. Casting herself as the spurned heroine and Bikram as the indifferent hero in one painting after another, she soaked in the pleasure of suffering, singing under her breath, 'I shan't fear you because you have come in the garb of sorrow.' As she walked along the wall, something else was happening. She seemed to have borrowed some of Esha's magic and Neelam's beauty to become a more complete woman. And she wanted to test her acceptance by Mahanam and Aritra. Only if she was a complete woman would she able to go up to Bikram in all her glory, her neck arched proudly upwards, and say, 'Look at me and tell me if you know who I am.'

To Esha, the entire experience of Ajanta was a miracle as well as agony. The work of any great artist is invariably multidimensional. This quality is achieved outside their knowledge and, sometimes, their devotion too. The Buddhist artists who had reverently depicted the story of Tathagata Sakyamuni's brotherhood with people could not have imagined even in their dreams that the magnificence of the superman would supplant the noble sorrow of his self-denial to an audience two thousand years from today.

Siddhartha's mother Maya stood leaning against a pillar. People said that she was rapt in thought after being informed that she was to give birth to a superman. But Esha saw the young woman weighed down by her unborn child, burdened by the imperative responsibility for a future yet to arrive. The superman was coming, but only by tearing her apart. She would have to leave her wonderful life marked by the gentleness of her husband Suddhodana and enriched by royal wealth, she would have to leave even the joy of imminent motherhood. Who knew with what intense pain.

Returning to Kapilavastu, Siddhartha has forced his half-brother, Gautami's son Nanda, to renounce the world too. Nanda's fianceé Janapadakalyani is slumped on her deathbed at the news. The messenger of defeat stands nearby, holding the discarded crown, while a tragic death seems to mock at the princess's countenance. Her eyes hold the blue darkness of a hundred centuries, her breasts are like distressed seashells—moist with milk—one of an ancient line of sensual women. In one cave after another, with faces as pale as those shells, cold hands the colour of miserable birds, women with saddened eyes seemed to follow Esha, reaching out to the sky to say—I want you. I want you. The echoes rang in Esha's empty womb, in the bare chamber in her breast. Sibali, Mahajanaka's wife, and Yashodhara of the heartbreaking eyes with Rahul in her arms. The dark-skinned princess with lowered eyes. Even the nymph Krishna flying in the sky was a heartrending melody. Sita's weeping, Rati's mourning, Radha's grief. Someone had come with unending promises, but not kept his word, leaving the earth empty as he left.

Esha could not decide what to name the intense feeling of pain that she was overcome by, which pierced her consciousness. But this sensation had not crushed her. Like a powerful ring of smoke rising from the soil, it bore her upwards into space, she would probably cross the ionosphere any moment, after which would come outer space and the company of innumerable stars and planets and satellites. Where an asteroid hurtling across space suddenly turned into a flaming comet, drawing a line of light on the canvas of emptiness, where the sun along with a cluster of planets circled in an eternal orbit, saying in a choked voice, let me reach, let me reach somewhere. O fate, hanging O almighty, the recurring nature of this revolution exhausts me, it exhausts me. You have created a path where one cannot even fall behind. The moving path moves itself and others according to its own rules.

These feelings had separated Esha from the rest, like the idiosyncrasy of a poet. It severed her from everyone, putting her in peril. Because unless one can travel in conjunction with the world, one's sense of security is destroyed. Esha felt as though the anguish of her loneliness had started eons ago. It could never belong to a single lifetime.

And yet at this very moment Mahanam was overpowered by an incomparable joy. Every footstep seemed to awaken, like the hundred-petalled lotus, the possibility of something priceless coming to him. *Agoham asmi loksas.* I am the first on earth. I am the first who will get it. But he did not know with certainty what it was. He did not want to know, either. The news of the discovery alone had so overwhelmed him, so inundated him, that he had pushed the joy to the background of his heart. He wanted to walk along the path of knowledge that he was accustomed to treading. He told his companions the detailed story of the Jataka tale preserved in each of the paintings. The stories of Compia-Jataka, Vishwantar-Jataka, the tale of Ourna and Bhabila. Sometimes the guide himself and other tourists stopped to listen. With a hand on a pillar, he explained the techniques of its creation step by step. The frescos at Ajanta, Michelangelo's The Last Supper on the ceiling of the Sistine Chapel, the Tun-Huang cave pictures of China. Why had prehistoric man chosen this particular cave for his sacred pursuit of art? The connection between artists lay in their choice of location. He also told of the extraordinary pleasure of viewing the paintings of Ajanta as a pictorial depiction of Kalidas's works. For, the period in which the art of Ajanta was created and the age of Kalidas—that is to say, the age of classical literature influenced by Kalidas—were more or less contemporary. The characters of *Kumarsambhava* and especially of *Meghdoot* seemed to have come alive in the caves under the artist's brush.

As Mahanam recited lines from *Meghdoot*, his sonorous

voice spread deep into the interiors of the cave. His joy created a halo of light around him, preventing him from noticing the changes in his companions' positions and emotions. Without being aware of Bikram's mocking glance, Seema's wistful restlessness, Neelam's repentance, Aritra's decision or Esha's grief, he paced about the world of Ajanta like a predatory beast. In his ears rang the cantos from the Bhattikavya, or, sometimes, the sounds from the sport of lions.

SIXTEEN

When they had finished their lunch after descending from the hills, Mahanam said, 'Let me stay another day. I was so busy with the panels that I didn't see the work on the ceiling closely. Some pictures, the façade of the caves—I have to see those too.'

'I don't feel like going back ever,' said Esha. 'I would have lain down in one of the viharas if I could have, with my head on a pillow of rock, spending my days on a bed of stone. I would catch a glimpse of Amitava every morning and evening, rapt in his joys and sorrows and meditation.'

Bikram said, 'Isn't there something called the Nivritti Marga? If you walk on that path, Esha-ji, thousands of householders will want to renunciate the material world. All the caves and sangharams and viharas will be packed with people. Don't even think of it.'

Neelam spoke intensely. 'I am an ignorant woman. What I have seen is enough. I shall go back, Aritra.'

'No problem, I'm definitely going back,' said Bikram

with great enthusiasm. 'Let Neelam Bhabi come with me. No need for the bus. I'm sure Chowdhury-da is staying back too.'

Aritra sensed trouble when Neelam said she would go back. He hadn't exactly come for Ajanta, he had come for Esha. He was not done with her. How could he go back, leaving her in Mahanam's care? Yet he could see that Neelam's decision to return would prove a challenge to him.

Bikram's question made it easier for him. 'Naturally,' he said. 'You can't be done with Ajanta in a day. Amateurs like us need two days at least. Especially when Mahanam-da's the guide, it would be silly to let the opportunity go. Why can't you stay another night, Neelam?'

'I've seen what I had to, understood what I had to, Ari,' said Neelam indifferently. 'Why don't you stay? I'm not stopping you. Let me go.'

'I'll drive very carefully,' said Bikram. 'Neelam Bhabi will have the entire back seat to herself, to sit or to lie down, as she pleases. Nothing to worry about. Besides, Seema will be there. So smart, so resourceful.'

Narrowing his eyes, Bikram patted Aritra on the back. Straightening, Aritra said, 'Is that what you'd prefer, Neelam?'

Neelam said, 'It's much better to go with Seema and Bikram than to travel such a long way alone on buses. I'm going, Mahanam-da. Enjoy the caves, Esha, I got a chance to visit Ajanta thanks to you. I haven't been here before though we live nearby.'

Neelam opened the car door and got in the back silently. Leaning back, she closed her eyes. Aritra bent over, his arms on the window.

'Aren't you feeling well, Neelam?'

'No, I'm very tired.'

'You've been working too hard, Neelam. Ever since my accident. Your maid merely pays a cursory visit. You must get the bai to do all the work, I insist. And we'll be back tomorrow.'

In her head Neelam said, you'll never come back, Aritra. I know. And there's no need to, either.

Aritra said, 'Phone Pupu as soon as you get back. Tell her to come home at once. Tell her we missed her a lot.'

Silently Neelam said, you won't have Pupu anymore, Ari. You have to pay a price too. I'll get a lot of time with her. Pupu's exams end tomorrow. Then Pupu and I will fill the empty house with a lot of things to tell each other.

The car left. But the last thing that Aritra had said kept ringing in Neelam's ears. Pupu, Pupe, who knew how her exams had gone? She'd been away from home only two days. But it felt much longer. Decades. Pupu was standing at a distance she could not bridge. A river flowed between them. What river? What was this river that could not be crossed? Was it the river of forgetting?

The sun didn't set till seven. There was still a little light. Esha had gone to the shop with the hope of buying souvenirs. She returned disappointed. 'You're making a mistake, Esha,' said Mahanam. 'The successors to the artists at the temples of Konark or Jagannath still live nearby, the memories of the originals are alive in their hands. You might get a replica of the Yakshi of Konark there. But here, there's been an interval of thirteen hundred years. It's all a mystery—who they were, where they went, why they went.'

With a sigh Esha said, 'Maybe they got their liberation, and now their art is getting its too. The great, ultimate liberation. Is the excess of renunciation in our country the reason for our decline? Buddhadeva not only withdrew from the material world himself, he also made every man with potential in contemporary India do the same. What harm would it have done if his brother Nanda had married Janapadakalyani and ruled the kingdom as Shuddhona's heir? He made Rahul become a monk too when he was just a boy, on the grounds that he was his father's property. Couldn't he have waited? I've heard that Ananda was his cousin. I can never consider this penchant among Kshatriyas for becoming a monk as beneficial to people. Chaitanya repeated the same history. What a powerful, cerebral, enlightened, heroic man he was, what an extraordinary blend of valour and knowledge. Could he not have fulfilled his duty to the country, to the nation, to people, with something other than his devotional songs and his trances? In modern times there was Vivekananda, he devoted himself to serving the poor, felt the need for courage. But again there was this gigantic festival across the country of creating monks and seers. So who were the people who remained in every age to create the next generation? The cunning enemies of Buddha, the corrupt Jagai and Madhai, and the decadent babus. And so we keep regressing every single day. Why be surprised that such an India gives birth to weaklings, cowards, traitors, opportunists and malicious people? Bhishma will never return, nor Rama or Lakshman or Bharat or the Pandavas, all of whom gave every drop of their blood for their country and people and society. Think about it, Rama and the Pandavas ruled their kingdoms even after the horror of leaving Sita or the Kurukshetra war—was it not for the sake of their subjects?'

Aritra said, 'Oh my god! What a lecture! Is this what you tell your students—with such passion? Is the life force of a nation banked with only a handful of people? In that case no real humans should have been born in post-war Europe.'

'Their poet himself has told us Aritra that post-war Europe was a dead land, that its people were the hollow men. Post-war history belongs not to Europe but to America. But I do not know what magic Germany used to absorb its enormous damage, to overcome the splitting of the country, to stand up again so heroically with its head held high.'

Mahanam said, 'There can never be only one reason for the degeneration of a country, Esha. India has always accepted defeat against external enemies because of its internal wars—Kauravas versus Pandavas, Ambhi versus Puru, Jaichand versus Prithviraj, Nehru versus Jinnah, and now, in recent time, Bhindranwale, Ghising . . . it goes on and on. Another big reason is the ancient practices of our caste-based social system. The Brahmin will only perform priestly tasks and teach, he will not know how to defend himself. The Vaishya will only be involved in agriculture and trade, he will not learn how to handle weapons. As for the Shudra, the less said the better. So in the event of being attacked, there will be no one but a handful of Kshatriyas to defend the country.'

Esha said, 'Even the Kshatriyas were taught to lay down their swords. In the Vishwantar Jataka the prince relinquished his weapons. The subjects had reason to be infuriated—they were intelligent.'

'It wasn't like this at the beginning, though,' said Mahanam. 'Dronacharya, Parasuram, Ashwathama were all merchants of war despite being Brahmins.'

Aritra said, 'But the Mahabharata spun plenty of tales to establish that they were exceptions.'

'They could also be the remnants of the original classless society,' said Mahanam. 'They acquired the caste system from the Dravidian civilization at Harappa. Before the Aryans came to India, their men, women and children could all use weapons. That was why they could destroy such a well-established Dravidian civilization despite being far less knowledgeable and far more impoverished. But this particular disease of civilized life attacked them too. The women threw down their bows and arrows to take up spoons and ladles. The boys exchanged their sticks for balls. As a result we have so much specialization now that the dentist cannot treat the ear.'

Mahanam jumped to his feet. 'Give me a few minutes. Let me do my exercises.' He went into his room, which he was sharing with Aritra. They were talking in Esha's room. The bed was on one side, and there was a desk and two chairs. Aritra and Mahanam were on the chairs and

Esha, on the bed, swinging her legs.

'Let me ask for some tea or coffee, all right?' said Aritra.

'All right,' said Esha.

When Aritra returned, Esha said, 'Do you remember Ari how you collected me at Hedua and took me to Mahanam-da's house in Duff Lane as a huge surprise? There was so much trouble and notoriety because Mahanam-da had superseded many of his seniors to become a professor immediately on his return from Oxford. Meanwhile the students were lapping up his lectures. Do you remember how I used to argue with him as an equal even though I was only an immature undergraduate?'

Aritra said, 'The best moment came when Mahanam-da dismissed Rabindranath's prose, and called Sudhin Dutta's writing stilted. You asked for an example of good prose, and he quoted from *The Religion of Man*. On the brink of being deceived, you won, jumping to your feet and clapping, saying, "Rabindranath, Rabindranath!" I can still see it.'

'How angry you were,' said Esha. 'Mahanam-da laughed and said no great writer can be rejected in entirety, I think it very artificial to create categories like so-and-so's prose or so-and-so's poetry. Think of it this way, *Vasundhara* is marred by too much dialogue, *Ashambhav* is a brilliant opera, the sermonizing in *Gora* is lifeless, the incomparable narrative has lifted *Noukadoobi* from a romance to a novel—what could have become another *Radharani* had almost become a *Chandrashekhar* instead.'

'You remember everything. How amazing,' said Aritra.

'Why shouldn't I remember Ari, it was Mahanam-da

who taught me how to apply the fundamental theories of literary criticism—those things were never taught in class. What do they teach besides the use of some vague terms? I might not agree with him on everything, but it was he who showed me the way. I should have asked Mahanam-da whether he's revised his opinion on "Vasundhara" as a poem and *Sahitya* and *Sahityer Pathey* as prose.'

Aritra said, 'Judging from the way he was reciting *Meghdoot*, it seems he quite likes emotion and hyperbole in poetry these days. Anyway, are we going to discuss Mahanam-da all the time, Esha? Don't we have anything to say about ourselves?'

Smiling, Esha recited:

Everywhere in life, in every song, there are things to say
But even after that words hold silence.

Esha had bathed before they had begun talking. She had been exuding a mild fragrance for a long time, as though from the era of Kalidas himself. Her thick hair was untied, billowing. Had she too dried her hair in incense smoke? Her hair as dark as Vidisha's ancient nights . . .

'No Esha, if you have indeed come after all these years, I cannot imagine that you have nothing to give me besides silence in words.'

Esha recited:

Perhaps I give, not poetry or song
But the tears of the bird with broken wings
An evening face to face like a massive star
An eternal fragrance

If nothing else, as far as the eye can see
Sunlight on the earth the colour of grain . . .

'I have given you so much, Aritra. The revival of old memories, forgiveness for an old injustice, imperishable friendship, what more can I give you?'

Aritra was almost on his knees. 'Please, Esha,' he said inarticulately.

'You want more?' Esha was not smiling. There was sadness in her eyes. Self-absorbed, she said distantly, 'I give you those silk-cotton trees without leaves or fruits, which shine like lighthouses even in glaring sunlight, I give you the grey dust on this pilgrimage, I give you the strange smile and sorrow on Amitava's face, neither of which I have understood properly, nor want to. What else do you want?'

Aritra had drawn Esha's feet, like tender silk-cotton leaves, to his breast—such soft, smooth, generous petals of feet. Rubbing his cheeks against them, Ari smothered them with kisses.

Esha turned stock still. Her eyes and eyebrows held astonishment. Withdrawing her feet roughly, she stood up, saying with anger and disappointment, 'Go away, Ari. Do you also think like Seema that you can do anything with me just because I am alone?'

'Why don't you understand?' said Ari softly. 'I have surrendered myself to you, I am surrendering to the first and last love of my life. I will take only as much as you give. You don't know how much of your life has been deposited with me, Esha. How will you be fulfilled if you don't have me?'

Esha said, 'Nothing but a past experience of mine lies with you, Ari. And that experience belongs to me. There is no question of my fulfilling myself by getting something from you. I came away long ago from the truth that existed between us. Try to understand, Ari, for me you're no different from my girlfriend Piku. There is no difference of gender in our relationship.'

Aritra said, 'My blood is testifying just the opposite. It couldn't be this way unless it was mutual. You're lying, Esha. It's just that you cannot reject your conditioning.'

'Absolutely not,' said Esha emphatically. 'If it had been a case of my conditioning, I would have told you as much. It's your vanity that won't let you admit that I have totally outgrown you, Ari. Even with an extraordinarily beautiful and talented wife like Neelam you're behaving like a beggar with me. How can you? Shame on you, Ari!'

'Alas, Esha, even with all her beauty and talents added and multiplied, Neelam cannot match up to you. How can I forget you!'

'Leave the room, Ari,' said Esha. 'I'm going to bed now. I'm not enjoying myself anymore, I'm not enjoying any of this. I have made an unpardonable mistake in coming here.'

Esha shut the door, not opening it the rest of the night, as though she was trying to leave no sign of herself behind the silent door. At dinner Mahanam said, 'What's this? Isn't she eating?' Aritra had tried in vain to talk to her from outside her door. 'She won't eat,' he said.

Mahanam said, 'Well then, it's just the two of us flickering in this huge dining hall. But I'm famished, and they do a delicious daal-bhaji here. Let's eat.'

In his bed at night, Aritra Chowdhury felt a menacing wind from the direction of Ajanta. A terrible, revengeful wind. His heart began to ache and swell in his chest, to a point where he felt it would burst out of his body. So this was how Esha had taken revenge? Arousing him in body, mind, and memory, making him clutch her feet in passion, and then throwing him away with skilful indifference. It was for this that she had come back eighteen years later. Wonderful! Lying in bed, Aritra could see his own humiliated face in the mirror. A mendicant Shiva with matted locks. Pounding and crushing him with her feet, the goddess Kali had hung dozens of heads of a dead Aritra around her neck, Esha was staring at her, stupefied.

Mahanam was not as much of a detached sage as Aritra had thought. When Esha didn't come down to dinner, and when he saw her door irrevocably shut while passing her room through the corridor, Mahanam had realized that something was wrong. And that Aritra was probably the cause. Coming out of his room very early in the morning, he found Esha walking down the stairs with her suitcase. She had bathed already, and tied her hair up. Dressed in a grey chiffon sari with floral prints, she was ready for the day. Startled by Mahanam, she came up to him quickly and said as though offering an explanation, 'I'm not going up to Ajanta, Mahanam-da. I stayed the night, that's all. I'm going to leave my suitcase at the counter and look around a little by myself.' After some hesitation, she added, 'I won't go back to Pune with the two of you either. I'll go to Bombay directly from Aurangabad. Then we'll see.'

'Sudden change of plans?' said Mahanam. 'What's the

matter, Esha?'

'Things get complicated wherever I go, Mahanam-da, that's just my luck.'

Mahanam said gravely, 'You ran away back then, this time too you're running away. Must Aritra Chowdhury win every time?'

Esha said regretfully, 'He's created a situation where Neelam will be very upset unless I go away. Didn't you see how she left yesterday? As though leaving the field clear for me, her condemnation written all over her face. But I'm not here to play. If Neelam doesn't understand this, how will Ari? Neelam has been deeply hurt by his behaviour. And it's all because of me.'

Mahanam said, 'No one can tell when sadness can prove useful to someone. And if Neelam suffers a bit because of you, that will settle accounts. What's the use of letting the poor woman be in your debt forever?'

Now Esha's heart broke, the tears welling up in her breast. She lowered her face in a desperate effort to stop them at her throat. Mahanam said, 'At that time you didn't dare come to me Esha, I had acquired a terrible reputation. If you can trust me this time, I'll be at your side. Join battle with Aritra. Don't run away from the battlefield. Unless you can break him once and for all you will not find release from one another.'

Esha stood with her back to him. Mahanam could make out that she was weeping in silence. Love had died. But its wounds were still fresh in some places. Mahanam had brought fresh pain to the raw welts. Esha was a young woman of nineteen now. Who had been used and discarded. Samiddha. The tilt of the flawless pearl-coloured neck, the stray wisps of hair near her ears. An infinitely gentle, infinitely suffering thing. Mahanam felt his hands trembling with sympathy. But she was also an independent spirited woman. He could not belittle her with consolation. She had to be given courage. More courage. When his own hands would no longer shake with hesitation, when they could be steady but be backed by his heart, then, only then would he have the right to offer her comfort in the form of courage.

'What was your original plan?' asked Mahanam.

'Go back to Pune, spend two days there, then go to Bombay, take the ship to Goa, return to Bombay and take the Geetanjali Express back to Calcutta. That's to say, I was supposed to. I bought my return ticket accordingly.'

'All right,' said Mahanam, 'I'm going to maintain your itinerary. I'm going to accompany you throughout, all the way back to Calcutta. I'm here. But it is you who'll have to fight the battle and win it, Esha.'

Having stayed up most of the night, Aritra could not stave off sleep at dawn. He had overslept. Getting dressed and going downstairs for breakfast, he found Mahanam drawn up to his full height near the door, smoking a long cigarette. White shirtsleeves rolled up, black-and-white checked trousers. Bathed, neat and clean, hair and beard perfectly in place. Aritra looked scruffy in comparison with his sleepless reddened eyes and a greenish stubble on his face. It was Neelam who kept him well-groomed, for Aritra's age-old habit was to crumple up his clothes and throw them away. Even when he was not in a hurry to go to office, Neelam went hoarse urging him to shave and bathe.

Mahanam sat down at the breakfast table with Aritra. Unfolding his newspaper, he said very casually, 'Oh yes, Ari, Esha was saying she won't go back to Priyalkarnagar. It seems she can make out you're finding it difficult with her there. Not enough space. I'd better make arrangements for her to stay at Chandrashekhar's house.'

Startled, Aritra said anxiously, 'What! Our plans are all worked out. Besides, Neelam will be terribly disappointed if she doesn't come back to our place. Please explain to her, Mahanam-da. Chandrashekhar's house is a bachelor's, how can she stay there?'

'So what? I don't think Esha cares for all that. And I'm there too. There won't be any problems. Chandrashekhar has enough space.'

'No, that's impossible. Esha, Esha!' Aritra leapt to his feet and went towards her room. He was knocking on the door. Mahanam smiled gently at his impatience.

Esha opened the door. Bowing his head, Aritra said, 'Forgive me this time, Esha. What explanation will I give Neelam if you go away somewhere else?'

It was nine at night by the time they got back to Pune via Aurangabad. Accompanying them to their doorstep, Mahanam left, refusing to go in.

SEVENTEEN

Giving up things is easy to promise, hard to achieve. Besides, deviating from routine increases the possibility of mistakes. Impulses don't last. Neelam returned to 233, Block B, Priyalkarnagar, and unlocked the door, fresh air filled the rooms soon after the windows were opened. The Marathi lady upstairs whom they had left the keys with had had the house cleaned every day. Neelam sprayed a freshener in every corner, switched the lights on, lit incense sticks. The surface of the table, the top of the chairs, the photograph of Goa on the wall all brightened. Neelam felt that she had had a delusional lapse of memory, for how else could she have considered this home, which she had built bit by bit herself with so much love, impure? She had come close to having her consciousness distorted by this distortion of memory, *smritibhrangsad buddhinasa*, saved only by remembering that a person perishes in that case, *buddhinasat pranasyati*. Pupu at eighteen was untainted, pure, sacred, how could she have considered introducing the poison of complications to her life? The first thing that Pupu had said when she had phoned was, 'Is Baba all right? He's not limping, is he?' 'Yes, come home, I'm back.' 'Why did you come alone Ma? Baba isn't fully fit yet, and besides, you know he's a bit cranky these days.' Neelam felt like asking, 'Doesn't your mother mean anything to you, Pupu?' But the question trembled on her lips and stopped. As it is Pupu would say, 'You're too sentimental, both of you.'

This time she was also on the verge of revealing the secret. 'You know, Pupu, your father isn't really your father. I was married earlier, you're my daughter from that marriage.' If she put it this way the impurity of the whole thing would go, but the hurt? The hurt would probably stay forever. Neelam could not gauge Pupu's possible reaction. But her paternal assets were so valuable that she should be informed. Actually Neelam's need was greater than Pupu's. The burden of the truth was so heavy that Neelam could not bear it alone anymore.

That's why Neelam breathed a sigh of relief when Esha and the rest of them returned. Aritra's first words on entering was, 'Where's Pupe?' Pupu came out of her room at once.

'You've lost so much weight in just two days, Baba. So sunburnt too.' Ari smiled, 'This is known as a peaches-and-cream complexion. Gets tanned easily. When was your father a white-skinned Englishman, Pupu? How did your exams go?' Meanwhile, Esha was telling Neelam, 'Dr Roy went back from the doorstep. I pleaded with him to come in for a cup of tea at least, but he refused.'

Pupu said, 'Won't you invite him home once more before

he goes back, Ma? Don't make too many items, else there's no time to talk.'

Esha saw that Neelam was looking stricken. And Neelam saw that Esha looked exhausted, dispirited. It had been very important to inform Neelam that Mahanam had been with them all the time, right up to the front door. Having discharged her duty Esha did not pause a moment longer. She went in for a bath. A shower. Let all the fatigue, filth, regret, be washed away by a clean stream of water.

Esha came out of the bathroom with wet hair. Pulling her hair-dryer out quickly, Pupu said, 'Do you wet your hair often when bathing, Esha Mashi? Dry your hair.' Making Esha sit down at her own desk, she stood behind her and ran the dryer herself.

'Do you use the dryer a lot?' asked Esha. 'It'll turn your hair grey quickly. That's why fashionable women grey early these days.'

'Oh, how I would love it,' said Pupu.

'Is everything about you upside down?' laughed Esha.

'Don't you see, Mashi?' said Pupu. 'It would make me look like Dr Mahanam Roy.'

Neelam started so violently that both Esha and Pupu turned towards her. Esha looked at Pupu, and then said, 'That's true, you do resemble Mahanam-da.'

'I must have been his daughter in some other life,' said Pupu. 'Although I don't believe in reincarnation.'

'Don't become too rigid about your beliefs so early in life, Pupu,' said Esha. 'You have no idea how many complex problems of life could be solved if there were such a thing as rebirth.'

Neelam was sitting as still as a corpse. Throwing a quick glance at her, Esha said:

I am at least thirty-five today
You are barely fifteen, and yet
The secret wound oozes the poison of memory
When I look at your young face

Neelam raised her eyes to look at them. They were brimming with tears. Pupu was listening closely to the poem, which Esha had recited in Bengali. 'The rhythm is lovely,' she said, 'but I understand Bengali poems only in translation. You used the word "gurho", what does it mean?'

'Secret.'

'The secret wound oozes the poison of memory. How lovely! You make beautiful poetry, Esha Mashi.'

'What I recite is always the work of others. This was Sudhindranath Dutta's translation of Heine's poetry.'

Neelam realized that Esha had come to know. Mahanam had never even considered staking a claim, but Pupu was bound to learn the truth some day or the other. It was best to let her find out for herself.

Esha didn't sit at the table to eat. Pupu took a glass of milk to her in the room. The three of them were having a family dinner after a long time. Aritra went to bed as soon as he had eaten. And fell asleep at once. Before going to bed, Neelam went into Pupu's room to find Esha missing. Searching for her, she finally located her on the fifth floor roof. The floor of the terrace was tiled. The sky appeared very near. The end of Esha's sari was fluttering in the gentle breeze.

'What is it Esha, you didn't go to bed?'

'I can't sleep. I've troubled all of you a lot, Neelam. Forgive me.'

'What do you mean? I should be thanking you. You've given us so much. Beautiful experiences, wonderful company, love, so many truths would have remained piled up had you not come. It's you who must forgive me if you can. I've only taken. When I try to give now, I don't find anything valuable enough.' Neelam was weeping.

Esha felt as though what Aritra should have told her was being channelled through Neelam. Because she needed to hear this. 'There's no need to suffer for the past, Neelam,' she said. 'It's a new day.'

Neelam said, 'The thing about Pupu made you sad all over again, didn't it?' Even as she said this, Neelam realized that despite her shame and sorrow, she felt a sense of pride. She had always got what she wanted. Her hands were filled with all she had got. Only Esha's hands were empty.

'It wasn't very unexpected,' Esha told her. 'We knew, all the students in our group knew, that you were Mahanam-da's. Everyone was surprised when things turned out differently.'

Neelam looked away. 'Now you know how terrible I am, Esha. You must hate me.'

Esha said, 'Would you make the whole thing clearer to me, if you don't mind? Was it your choice? Aritra instead of Mahanam-da? Or was it Mahanam-da who didn't want to accept you and his child?'

'Mahanam-da has come to know about his child today, eighteen years later. I decided not to let him know, lest he stop me. The choice was mine. The responsibility was entirely mine. Ari had told me many things about Mahanam-da, which turned me away from him. And besides, you know his irresistible ways of making love. He can win over any woman of any age. If he wants to.'

After a long pause Esha said, 'He cannot win me over anymore, Neelam, you must trust me about this.'

'I know he can't. But that he wants to is my humiliation, don't you see?'

'No, it's not your humiliation,' said Esha. 'You've given him too much importance. Ignore him a little, deprive him. Fight. Don't let him win every time. For that's when it will be a resounding defeat for him.'

Neelam said, 'The one who wanted to deprive him has done it already. I have no womb, no eggs, I am a woman without womanhood.'

'I've heard,' said Esha. 'Why are you agonizing over this medical, this physiological fact? I'm saying you're still a woman. And, over and above that, a human being. Neelam, you must deprive him of what one person cannot do without from another. Don't let your charity be so unrestricted.'

'I'm not doing it anymore. I won't. I understand many of my mistakes now, which I hadn't earlier. That's why I was thanking you. But what do I give you, Esha? My heart is parched.'

Esha said emotionally, 'This is my biggest gift from you. However far I go away, your bounteous feet will always walk with me.' It was a new vow beneath the starlit night.

Aritra did not know. But the battle had begun. All the

cannons were trained on him. They were concealed behind the trees. Hidden eyes kept him under surveillance. The cavalry patrolled from a distance. You don't know, Aritra Chowdhury, that you are in serious trouble.

Neelam said, 'Bikram and Seema have requested us again and again. We're staying at their house in Bombay.'

Agitated, Aritra said, 'Phone them immediately and cancel it. I've made arrangements at the company guest house.'

Neelam said, 'They're waiting for us. I cannot hurt them. Why don't you stay at the guest house? I'll stay with the others at their house.'

'So you've made up your mind.'

'There's nothing to make up my mind about. They've invited us. They'll have made arrangements. Why should I turn them down?'

'You'll turn them down because Bikram's vulgarity crosses all limits sometimes.'

'I'm the vulgar type too, I can handle it.'

'You can't handle anything. The truth is that you like vulgarity. You've been indulging Bikram for a long time now.'

'I don't know whether I like vulgarity, but I do like a warm welcome. I admit it. The way Seema takes care of us when we go, the way Bikram is always ready to help, is not to be dismissed. And maybe I'm indulging Bikram, but who's indulging you?'

'Does my behaviour also reveal a vulgarity like Bikram's?'

'You've probably gone one better than him.'

Aritra was on his feet. Extremely agitated. About to say something offensive, he stopped. Had Esha said anything to Neelam? His face turned blue.

Pupu said, 'I was in Goa just the other day. I'm not going again. I'll stay back at Bikram Kaku's house.' Neelam decided that she would too, but there was no need to tell Aritra right now. She had to give him a lot of rope.

EIGHTEEN

Seema had had a lotus pond built on the terrace. Her parents' home in the Hooghly district of West Bengal had lotuses and water lilies. Land was very expensive in Bombay. And so the garden was on the open terrace. The wardrobes were packed with new nightclothes and dressing gowns for the guests. Bikram had made both his cars available round the clock. You never know where someone might want to go.

'Such attention to guests, this is incredible, Seema,' said Esha.

Seema said, 'A guest is an *atithi*, who arrives unexpectedly instead of adhering to the appointed date or *tithi*. You can visit me without luggage next time, Esha-di.'

Mahanam was astonished by the library and the collection of paintings and sculptures in Seema's house. Any album he wanted was available. Including those of Ajanta. He didn't have so many himself. Mahanam sketched to his heart's content along with Pupu. They would be used in his book, with due acknowledgement to Seema Seal and Samiddha Chowdhury.

Mahanam asked, 'Whose passion is all this, Seema?'

'No one's, Mahanam-da,' smiled Seema. 'Just one of the different ways of spending black money. We bought all this personally in the expectation that you would set foot in our house one day. Can't you see, there's not a mark on the golden embossing, no one opens the pages.'

'Why do you have to display so much humility, Kakima?' asked Pupu. 'Are you cultivating it deliberately? Seema Kakima has many interests, many talents, Dr Roy, she is extremely accomplished. But she refuses to acknowledge them. Sherlock Holmes said modesty is not a quality, it's another name for hypocrisy. Tell her, will you?'

How would Seema tell them that without acknowledgement and praise from the right quarters all talents become useless. Even if she did, Pupu would not understand. She did whatever she liked, all by herself, without caring for recognition or acclaim from anyone. Was this unique to Pupu, or a natural trait in women of the new generation? It needed observation. Seema would be very pleased if it was the latter. In her old age, as the wife of the chairman of some corporation or the other, she would mention this quality of the new generation at the conferences she would grace as a garlanded chief guest, asserting unequivocally that it was a sign of progress.

The street food vendors on Chowpatty beach were pestering Seema. Pupu was matching strides with Mahanam, an ice cream in her hand. Esha refused to lag behind. Neelam was walking next to Aritra in a white sari and blouse, Aritra was limping a little. Bikram said, 'What a dress, Bhabi! You look beautiful. But Chowdhury-da has been widowed.'

Neelam couldn't contain her laughter. 'You need to be widowed too,' she said. 'Seema will dress this way tomorrow.'

Esha wasn't speaking. She hadn't said a word since they had returned from Aurangabad, only offering monosyllables in answer to questions.

'Are you ill, Esha?'

'No.'

'Not depressed anymore?'

'No.'

'We're taking the ship to Goa, you'll love it. You haven't been to Goa before, have you?'

'No.'

'Are you unhappy?'

'Yes.'

'Are you angry with me?'

'No.'

'The anger's gone?'

'Yes.'

Pupu said, 'You people are walking very slowly, Baba. Dr Roy says he wants to see the Viceroys enter through the Gateway of India. Esha Mashi is saying she's seen the Elephanta Caves already, she's not in the mood to go again.'

Bikram said, 'Esha-ji has to be dunked in the sea at Juhu beach. Her mood will improve at once.'

'If I go into the sea I won't come out again, I'll go back to where I belong,' said Esha.

'You've come from the seabed?' asked Seema. 'Are you Lakshmi or Urvashi, Esha-di?'

'Neither Lakshmi nor Urvashi,' said Esha sadly. 'I'm a poison pot, Seema.'

'Neither a mother nor a wife, so far as I've heard not a daughter either, who can you be but Urvashi,' Bikram told himself.

Aritra said in his head, 'A man's heart loses itself suddenly. His blood pounds, Urvashi from heaven.'

Mahanam said, 'It's a matter of choice, Esha, whether you want to be Urvashi or Lakshmi.'

'I don't want to be either, Mahanam-da,' said Esha. 'Doesn't imagination offer any alternatives?'

'It does,' answered Mahanam. 'Instead of a poison pot, you could be a nectar pot. What do you want to be, Samiddha?'

'I don't want to be nectar either,' said Pupu. 'It would bore me stiff to be immortal, much better to be a bubble, full of colour and death.'

Mahanam recited:

O wide river
Your water, unseen, unheard
Uninterrupted, incessant
Flows eternally

'Look, Esha, Neelam, you can't blame god. Man wanted death voluntarily. Not with pique, but with love. Not like Freud's Thanatos, the death-wish which is a synonym for hatred—but with the kind of romantic passion that Pupu expressed. So there was death. And then, suffering from amnesia, he forgot that this was what he had wanted. He was furious. He made up all sorts of stories. Since then man has been at loggerheads with god.'

'So you accept an anthropomorphic god, Mahanam-da,' said Aritra. 'A god in the mould of humans, with arms and legs. God made man in his own image, and man returned the compliment.'

Mahanam said with a smile, 'You don't even get rhetoric these days, Ari, have you turned completely into an officer in a commercial firm then, aren't you a poet anymore?'

'Ari was never a poet, Mahanam-da,' said Neelam. 'He had the gift of the gab, that's all. And in youth even a bitch is a nymph.'

Esha said, 'Ari-da was not a poet? It's possible. Bikram was a singer too once upon a time. Now he manages his own enterprise, Ari-da manages someone else's.'

'What rubbish, I still sing,' protested Bikram vehemently.

'You may sing,' said Seema, 'but you're not a singer anymore.'

'What!' said Bikram incredulously.

Esha spoke little, and when she did, it was with Pupu, with Neelam, with Seema, with Mahanam, even with Bikram. But Ari was left out. Ari was left out.

But what had he done? Nothing. Nothing at all. At one time he had meant everything to Esha. He had all the rights in the world over her. Esha-Presha would melt like butter on his breast. Wouldn't she? Her hands and feet, lips and breasts were all made of soft wax, a wax that turned liquid under Aritra's passion. It was he who had made Esha who she was. She belonged to a conservative family. Esha would say, 'You know, Ari, among my cousins the girls are like roses or jasmines, the boys are all fair-skinned. I'm the only dark, ugly one. My aunt has been making me use beauty lotions from my childhood. But beauty never came.' Sometimes she would say, 'You know, Aritra, my cousins have their noses buried in thick books all the time. *Human Destiny*, *Religion Without Revelation*, *The Cosmic Blueprint*. Counting the number of scholars in this family will make your head reel. While I'm an ignorant fool, Aritra.' Esha would laugh. But through her laughter Aritra could hear the weeping of a girl constantly criticized.

From a distance he had seen a big car leaving the Khans' house, carrying several bejewelled fairies. Each of them with hair as black as queen bees, eyes like lotus petals, a nose like the softest of flowers, mouth and lips like ripe red fruits. Their faces demanded individual attention, their expressions were haughty, they never walked on the streets. Ravishing, they were. But no one would be inspired by their appearance to write poetry. There was Esha, coming out of the house. A willow tree. The huge front gates of the Khan mansion seemed to bow to her before closing. People all around. Cars speeding by. But Aritra could see no one else, there was no one else. Photographs don't come out well without appropriate backgrounds, such as a temple in a narrow lane. But how perfectly Konark stood amidst a desolate emptiness of sand stretching to the horizon, in all its glory. The perspective of a conservative, blind aristocracy. A meaningless procession of innumerable faces and cars in the backdrop. Esha approached, charged with meaning. The immortal woman.

Will she sleep alone this stormy night
Crawling expectantly in the blind lane
Imprisoned in her mother's watery womb
Where's the surgeon on this dreadful night?
Wait in the yard with the conch-shell
Let the sound mingle with its echo
Can there be an explosion of words
Will she awaken? Will she bring a ransom?

Aritra had given birth to Esha, hadn't he? '*Urrr naagin, laach naagin, laach naagin, laach*.' The snake had danced to the rhythm of the snake charmer's flute at the University Institute folk festival. Memories of earlier lives had flashed before her eyes. Well then? Did the incomparable Galatea whom he had built with his own hands not belong to Pygmalion anymore, did she belong to the entire world now?

Aritra tore his hair out, sank his teeth into his hands, biting them like the crocodile in the fairy-tale. Then, bleeding profusely, he died. And, in a laughing procession over this death they walked with their luggage up the gangway to The Condor, bound for Goa—a heroic Bikram, a brightly smiling Mahanam, a detached, distracted Esha-Presha; and in orange slacks, orange lipstick, orange nail-polish, and with an orange bag on her shoulder, a shiny Seema wrapped like a lozenge, and, bringing up the rear, a limping Aritra Chowdhury forced to rise to his feet and dust himself off.

NINETEEN

The steamer sounded its horn. The Condor would now unfurl its gigantic wings and fly across the wide sky of the Arabian sea. Like dolls—although they weren't dolls—ranged along the railing on the deck, stood Seema, Aritra, Mahanam, Bikram, Esha.

Why hadn't Neelam come? Despite all the cajoling and imploring? Beseeched to join the travellers, why did she still remain, impenetrable, on the distant shore they had left behind? The waves in the wake of the steamer were turning the blue water white. As frothy as a waterfall. As fearsome as a whirlpool. As though the water was playing the cymbals of death with both its hands. Why hadn't Neelam come? Esha was afraid. Was it just because of Pupu? Pupu was even more comfortable than Seema's son Tito in Bikram's house. Tito visited once a year, but Pupu went as often as she liked, for as long as she liked. Without her parents. Sometimes with her friends. And yet Neelam hadn't wanted to come. As though, clasping Pupu to her breast, she had bid goodbye to Aritra forever. Had Neelam left Ari for good? She was supposed to have fought, she was supposed to have lived with deprivation, but the question of abandoning him had never arisen. Ari had not understood. How terrifying! Esha could understand, but Ari was too besotted to realize that the ground beneath his feet was shaking. That he was floundering in bottomless water. He hadn't realized. Neelam, Neelam, you have been cruel to many people, directly, indirectly. Don't do it anymore. You must not pick up the scales of the blindfolded goddess of justice. You cannot be the deity who judges. Don't be. Esha seemed to be knocking her forehead against an uninterested Neelam's feet while Neelam stood in an empty sky. And The Condor kept flying regally, holding people in the span of its wings and in its beak. People who could neither stop the ring from whirling, nor escape it with a tremendous leap. Their actions had pinned them to the rim. Not because of their karma from another lifetime, but from this one. This one alone. And all of them, almost all of them, were silently adding the blue of their agony to the blue of the ocean with its restless waves. No one could see how the Arabian sea was turning darker in consequence. Currents of blood, blue in colour, were spreading from one coast to another. Charged with an electric force. So powerful was this blue stream of pain and desire that it would silently suck in anyone who fell into it.

Pointing with her wistful orange arm, Seema said, 'There, Esha-di. Flying fish. There's another, and another!'

Looking out of the corner of his bloodshot eyes, Ari saw a seagull swoop down on the water and pick up a fish in its beak. His heart leapt into his mouth, he shivered. He looked at Esha from a distance. She wasn't looking in his direction. What was she gazing at, so engrossed, so blue? Had she never seen the sea or water before? Had she never seen blue or green or white? Or was she gazing at all this so as to not look at him? Her eyes were riveted.

The colour of the day deepened. You couldn't look at the sea. Sharp knives flashed in its swells, there were fewer waves here at a distance from the harbour, the swaying was far less, but still it was a rough sea.

Esha sat in the dining hall with tomato soup and dry toast. Aritra was nauseous, Seema had opened her trove of delicacies. Bikram was eating, Mahanam was eating. Seema was watching, eating. Esha was eating with concentration. Aritra toyed with his food. What was Esha eating with such attention? Had she never tried tomato soup with dry toast before? Or would she not look at him, would she never look at him again, which was why she was eating this way, with heart and soul?

Esha and Seema were chatting with a family on the upper deck. An animated conversation. He couldn't tell whether they were Punjabis. Two fat-cheeked children, the woman was probably the same age as Seema. She was dressed in a churidar and kurta, Seema was talking to her, Esha was smiling, she got up and left, she was going towards the stern of the ship, what would she do if Ari followed her? She would certainly move towards the bow, if Ari went upstairs she would go downstairs, if he went lower she would go higher, much higher, much further, the gulf between them kept widening. Their journey from Pune station to Priyalkarnagar on that cool, pleasant night was so far behind them now, on the Siddheshwar Express from Kalyan to Pune, Aritra standing, Esha sitting, somehow they had found a seat for her. Many passengers between them. But still they were not far apart. Esha's cheeks were visible, sometimes her forehead, perhaps half her face, but still she was Esha, entirely Esha. But now, her body wrapped in a pink sari, Esha was moving constantly, indefatigably, sitting, standing, in his view, but this was Esha in fragments. She had no smile on her face for Ari, no eyes for him. One of Ari's eyes told him the separation was complete. The other said—impossible, this is impossible.

Mahanam sat in a deck chair, lighting his pipe. A fragrant smell. He had been immersed in the *Avadanasataka*, legends about Buddha and Ashoka, all afternoon. With the sun setting he had put his book away and lit his pipe. When he saw Aritra coming up to him he said, 'Want to taste my tobacco, Aritra, Bikram? I have a dozen pipes in my suitcase. Should I get them?'

'Not a very strong smell, Dada,' said Bikram. 'My brand is Charminar. Sometimes a Capstan. I don't care for Dunhill or anything like that. Can I say something, Dada? Shall we have some Scotch? Along with Goan seer cooked in wine and fried chicken liver. I'll make arrangements.'

'Why not?' said Mahanam. 'All right, Aritra?'

Aritra's breast was splitting with thirst, his heart arid. Can you lend the Gobi desert a rain-bearing cloud? He said, 'So be it. But don't get too drunk.'

Bikram left for his cabin with great enthusiasm, bringing Seema's case. A portable icebox and the liquor were inside.

Snacks to go with the drinks in a hotbox.

'Cheers, cheers!' The glasses were emptied rapidly. The evening passed. Night fell. Cheers, cheers. Deckhands in uniform walked past them. Vendors offered biscuits, coffee, nuts, cashews, cold drinks. Cheers, cheers. Kissing the bottle, Bikram said, 'Well, Chowdhury-da, am I drunk?' He was slurring his words a little. Aritra had to drink a lot. He was used to drinking very slowly. He was lively now, but not drunk. 'Ten highballs, right?' he said. Right now he was avoiding reality. Later, he would start slurring too. His limbs would give way, he would start talking, talking far too much, and then . . . ?

Bikram said, 'Then, fuck it, I'll die. Fall to the ground with a thump, the undertakers will drag me away by my feet. Roy-da, my Roy-da. Won't you save me? What's this, the girls aren't drinking. As if they don't. My wife drinks, she's shy because all of you are here. She turns into something else when she's drinking. Tight as a whip. Crisp fried prawns. Crunchy. Ray-da, you may be a bachelor, but you're not celibate, are you?'

Mahanam said laughingly, 'It seems you want to bare your heart. Go ahead, do it.'

'That's not it, Dada. I like you a lot. No pretence like Chowdhury-da here. Have you ever tasted a Santhal woman, Dada?'

Mahanam burst into laughter. 'This question must have been lurking in your mind for a long time. The alcohol has loosened your tongue today.'

'Not alcohol, Dada, whisky. Don't laugh, all right? No laughing matter. Santhal women best. Sophisticated women not like them. No, never. I challenge you. Fight. Prove it. I, Bikram Seal, I've tasted them all. I'm telling you. Adivasi women sexiest. All the sisters are here. Ask them. Hey, Seema.'

Aritra slapped Bikram coldly. Mahanam said, 'Empty the rest of the bottle on his head.'

Aritra said, 'Should I? Really? No one will be happier to do it than me.'

'Coffee! Here,' said Mahanam.

Bikram had an attack of hiccups. Mahanam poured the Scotch out of his glass and poured coffee into it. 'Drink this like a good boy, Bikram Seal,' he said.

Seema and Esha were downstairs, they were coming up the stairs now. Seeing the state Bikram was in, Seema hurried up to them. 'Oh god, you've spoilt the evening. Did you have to drink so much again? Can you support him from the other side, Ari-da, let's put him in the cabin, or he'll create a scene.'

'Ari and I will take him, you'd better go,' said Mahanam.

Esha wasn't even looking this way. She seemed to be walking in a dream. As though there was nobody here, no one else. To the right or to the left, in front or behind, there was nobody else on this ship. As the night deepened, the wind picked up speed. It was difficult to sit here. The deck was emptying out. Those who had cabins had entered them. The doors couldn't be opened against the wind. Despite his reluctance, Aritra had drunk so much that he was sleepy. Like a limp fly-whisk he had slumped on his bed. As he sank into sleep, he tried to find something through a dream. Dreams could not be dictated. Desiring to dream of Vivekananda or Sri Aurobindo, you could easily dream of dragons instead. So, instead of a pleasurable dream, Aritra was having a nightmare. An accident. Not on land, but on the water. His personal ship had shattered, the frame coming apart on both sides. The bow, the stern, the deck were all crumpling, falling into the sea.

Was that someone banging on the door! The wind? Aritra roused himself emphatically. Esha, Esha, after making me suffer so much, have you come to me finally? Have you? Aritra opened the door with his eyes closed. 'Seemachal, what is it?' As soon as Seema entered the wind whipped the door shut. Seema's eyes were blazing. 'Where's Bikram?' she asked. 'My Bikram? Where have you taken him?'

'Bikram? What are you saying, Seema? How should I know? Why should I have taken him anywhere?'

'What else can it be? I made him lie down with such care. As soon as I fell asleep for a bit, I find he's disappeared. He was prepared to stray, Ari-da, and you had already got him drunk and out of his senses by letting loose your beautiful wife and your sexy girlfriend on him. Did you have to add alcohol? What else is this but abandoning him? Now he's gone off in search of someone. Someone else. He doesn't want me anymore. Doesn't want me, doesn't want me.'

Seema flung herself on Aritra's chest, weeping uncontrollably. 'What will happen to me, then? What will happen to me?'

Standing ramrod straight, Aritra switched the light off in the cabin and told himself with a cruel heart, 'That's right. Why not this? All women have the same body in the dark. It's the same tree. The same flowers and fruits, the same roots and hollows. The main thing was hunger. Desire, desiring strongly with everything in one's life.' And so in that terrible darkness all the orange colours on Seema's body were shed and tossed away, and so in that icy darkness Seema's arms were torn out, legs were torn out, breasts were torn out. Filling the entire canvas, Picasso began to paint the Guernica of the civil war with twisted, mangled body parts, crying and burning, including the final whimpering cry of the dying she-horse. Drinking Seema, filling himself up to his throat, it was Esha whom Aritra drank. Drank with the thirst of the desert. He poured Esha into his goblet and drank her, dipped his brush into Esha's colours, he painted. Through Seema's body Aritra struggled with all his strength to overcome Esha's eternal resistance. But as soon as he sensed Seema's unique existence in the bitter, astringent taste in the heart of his heart, his soul screamed, 'There's no Esha, no Esha, Esha is an illusion, Esha is a mirage.' His body trembled with despair. Throwing Seema away from him, unfinished, he stood up, wobbling like a blind man. 'What is it Ari-da, what happened?' asked Seema, her voice thick with tears. Aritra's face was twisted, flooded by the grief of losing his beloved. Heartache, defeat, sorrow. Aritra could find his own voice no more. He groaned:

I cried for madder music and for stronger wine,
But when the feast is finished and the lamps expire,
Then falls thy shadow, Cynara! the night is thine;
And I am desolate and sick of an old passion,
Yea, hungry for the lips of my desire:
I have been faithful to thee, Cynara! in my fashion.

TWENTY

'You were drinking too, Mahanam-da, I saw,' said Esha. 'Weren't you?'

'Yes of course I did. I drank quite a lot. I've been drinking since I was twenty-one. It doesn't affect me at all. I don't get drunk. I have no addiction. See this pipe? I can give it up in an instant if you tell me to.'

'Really?'

'Really? All it does is help me think. Like they say, smoking out the ideas. But habits can be changed.'

'My life is devoid of men, you see. I don't trust these male entertainments that you people indulge in. May I sit here safely?'

'Considering I called you here, how can you not? Can I ask you something personal, Esha?'

'Of course.'

'Why is your life so devoid of men, anyway? Why did you leave that gentleman? Was he a very bad man?'

'No Mahanam-da, not at all.'

'What was it, then?'

'Whatever went wrong was always my fault. Amidst a crowd of people, my own habits make me aloof.'

'Tell me what these habits of yours are.'

Esha remained silent. And remained silent. Much later she said in a small voice, 'He was a very mechanical man. I'd accepted that too. But then he wanted to be a father.'

'Was that wrong?'

'No, it wasn't.' Esha lifted her eyes, looking through Mahanam, at the wall behind him. 'Not wrong. But I'm not just a womb.'

'You're right, Esha,' said Mahanam. 'When the world needed to add more people, the idea that motherhood is the ultimate fulfilment was ingrained in women. Society no longer has this need, womanhood should not be equated with motherhood anymore.'

'I don't know about that,' Esha said, 'all I know is that unless my heart is full, an exhausting mechanical act will not fill my womb. I cannot give birth to a child that way. I could not. Can a unique creation like Pupu come from a factory, tell me.'

Mahanam looked sharply at her. He put his pipe down beside the ashtray. 'Do you know the history of Pupu's birth?' he asked.

'I do.'

'Did you know beforehand?'

'No. Only a few days ago.'

'Why are you crying, Esha?'

Esha looked up. 'But I'm not.'

'I feel you're crying, trembling.'

'I'm not crying. Not trembling either, believe me. Why

couldn't you hold on to Neelam?'

'Perhaps I didn't want to strongly enough. I was quite immature myself then. Neelam was the only woman whom I could touch without sinning.'

'Meaning?'

Mahanam smiled. 'The history of my birth is also something like Pupu's. She has parents. I have no antecedents. The person who gave me her affection and property, Dr Kasturi Mitra, was not really my aunt. She had brought up an abandoned child in a hospital. Whenever a woman appeared attractive to my young eyes, I used to imagine that my unmarried mother had given birth to her after getting married. Or perhaps my father. In which case that woman was my sister.'

'You didn't think that way about Neelam?'

'No. She was Kasturi Mitra's friend Savitri Joshi's daughter. Savitri married a Gujarati. I knew Neelam's background through and through. And Kasturi Mitra had told me that my mother was a Bengali woman whom she did not know.'

'Do you know how old she was?'

'Not a particularly tender age.'

Esha said, 'My mother died while giving birth to me at just sixteen. I was a caesarean baby. My mother was rent apart giving birth to me. There is no way I can be your sister, Mahanam-da.'

'And your father?'

'Do you want to know my entire genealogy? My father observed perfect widowhood for three or four months. He didn't eat meat or fish, dressed in white cotton only.

When anyone asked, he said, "If I had died this is what you would have forced her to do. So I'm doing it."'

'And then?'

'Unable to bear it anymore, he willed himself to die. The larger family brought me up.'

'Which means you too are the creation of pure love. And you were born when your mother was sixteen, before she was even of marriageable age. Like Draupadi or Sita, you too have come out of moist earth.' Mahanam sat up. 'And this is the immaculate whom Aritra rejected.'

'Aritra was probably not to be blamed,' Esha said softly.

'What do you mean?'

'I realize it now. Aritra is the kind of man who cannot tolerate a second sun in the sky. He has to be the one and only. I did not understand, but his soul had understood that I was breaking out of his spell, the spell of his words, very rapidly. Thanks to your company. Gradually I shed the lies from my life and leaned towards the truth. Towards you. *Asato ma sadgamay*. Lead me from the unreal to the real.'

'Really?'

'Yes, that was probably why he took Neelam and tried to break both you and me together.'

The wind had thrown Mahanam's shawl into disarray. Esha said, 'When Ari left me at that time, I must have been furious. My self-confidence, my faith in the world, my pride, all of it was in pieces. But even before you recognized me, it was I who went to you first, with all the questions in my life, expecting correct answers. When you ignored me and chose Neelam, what I felt was the dirge written in the Padavali—my shrine is empty. Although I had not understood its nature then. But my work, my studies, living, Aritra's flattery, all of it tasted bitter. Nothing felt good, Mahanam-da, nothing.'

What she said about Mahanam began to widen like a ripple in water. My shrine is empty, my shrine is empty.

Mahanam said intensely, 'It was to fill your shrine that I have kept mine empty all these years. Is there anyone who cannot recognize the first one, the eternal one? If she is still not desired, it is only because history and myth create a treacherous gulf in the middle. I'm thirsty for nectar, but I quench my thirst with other things. Esha, you are my pitcher of nectar which came out of the churning of the seas.'

Mahanam's passion was stronger than the passion of the sea. He spread himself out wider than its waters. He was loftier than the waves. His body pulsated to a sense of expectation, but what he got was far beyond even those expectations. In astonishment he saw that this was not Praxitales's generously endowed Aphrodite with formidable thighs, the contours of whose headless body of inanimate stone were so alive that viewers still ran up to embrace her. He saw—how perfect!—that this was Sandro Botticelli's Venus, whose entire body was made of the light and shade of suggestive poetry. *Sa* Esha. She is this woman. Esha *sa*. This woman is she. Balanced on pearls like teardrops in an ocean of desire, she stood with her face pointing upwards. Because her feet were on the ground and her face was in the sky, no one understood her. As in the Egyptian imagination, a body of clay and heart of fire. Her expectations were not to be met by earth or fire or the world or the sky alone. She was shrouded in linen like a mysterious melancholy. Her promise was unfathomably deep. He would never be able to measure it. He could never reach its shores. One wave after another crashed on his familiar boats, setting them adrift. With a broken rudder and ripped sail, he set off on an exquisite voyage to an unknown destination. He had an abundance of supplies, but he himself would never be equal to this journey.

Mahanam had fallen asleep. His right arm was stretched out. He was sleeping with his head resting on it. His face held the intimacy of death. An enormous release. Setting his other arm back on the bed with a liquid fondness, Esha sat up. Outside, she realized that in the final phase of its journey, The Condor was speeding along like a rocket. Thousands of waves were breaking the sky into pieces with its clouds and stars and planets. The water of the Arabian sea was boiling in bubbles around the ship. The deck was sunk in the glow from the sky, as though a cascade of water was flowing over it. Only a handful of chairs were floating, like pieces of wood in an ocean. Floating away, then floating back.

Resting her hands on the railing, Esha asked the sea and sky, whom shall I give my wealth, then? It will not run out even if I give it away with ten hands instead of two. Will something of me always be left over? Forever? What sort of cruel fate is this?

At that precise moment, as her nameless yearning rose from her intense sadness at feeling incomplete, someone on the deck of The Condor touched her from the back with a hand of air, calling out to her sonorously.

Esha felt goose pimples on her skin. Her veil trembled. All her resistance willed itself to fall away. If she turned around to look, she would burn with the unbearable joy of seeing him. Balling her fists, she tried with all her strength to restrain her heart, her lungs, her blood-bearing veins and arteries, all of which wanted to leap out of her body. Finally she turned around. There was no one there. It was empty. The top deck was absolutely empty at midnight. But she was certain that someone had come. No one she knew. And yet someone she had known for a long time. An indistinct form, his garments of uncertain colour, a deep, masculine fragrance. Had he left faster than the wind?

Restlessly she went downstairs. Wrapped from head to toe in blankets and sheets, whatever she could find to guard against the extreme cold, the passengers on the upper deck were swaying with the ship. Sleep all around her, only sleep. Rows of men, women and children were deep in sleep. A few young men had been trying to huddle behind a sheet and play a game of cards. They too were asleep, with the cards strewn around. A deckhand in uniform was passing. In desperation she asked, 'Did you see anyone climb down here?'

'I thought I saw someone, he went to the lower deck.'

'The lower deck?' It wasn't very easy to go there. Every inch was covered with people. And this terrible wind on top of it. But she had to go. The lower deck was even more crowded. The assault of the wind was less here, though. Esha scanned almost every single person. Like the widows of the brave warriors searching for their husbands' corpses on the battlefield after the Kurukshetra War. But Esha knew he wasn't dead, he was exceptionally alive, he had made her feel an ecstasy that still pulsed in her. He knew, too, that she was searching for him. But there was no need to scour the ship for him, for she would be electrified as soon as she went near him. And so she went back to the upper deck, and then up the stairs to the top deck adjoining their cabins.

The night had lightened by then. Clouds of different shapes were becoming recognizable in the sky. Slowly the nocturnal wind was bringing itself under control. The birds on the shore would soon wake up and begin their song. Opening the door of his cabin, Mahanam came out to discover a dishevelled, sleepless Esha standing with her hands on the railing. With her back to him. Going up to her, he found her face awash with tears. 'Haven't you slept, Esha?' he asked.

Esha turned. 'Someone made me rapturous and left,' she said.

'Who was it? What was it?' Mahanam asked in surprise.

'I don't know. I looked for him all night. Lower, even lower. See, I still have goosepimples.'

Mahanam listened with close attention. Night was breaking into dawn. The sky was neither black nor blue. Colourless, luminescent. Looking at it, he said, 'Why search any more, Esha? Don't you understand? You've found him. Found him already. He will flow in your blood from now on, sing in your blood. He will take all you have to offer without emptying you out, and will return it to you with thousand times the ecstasy. Can a pilgrimage ever fail, Esha?'

A NOTE ON THE AUTHOR

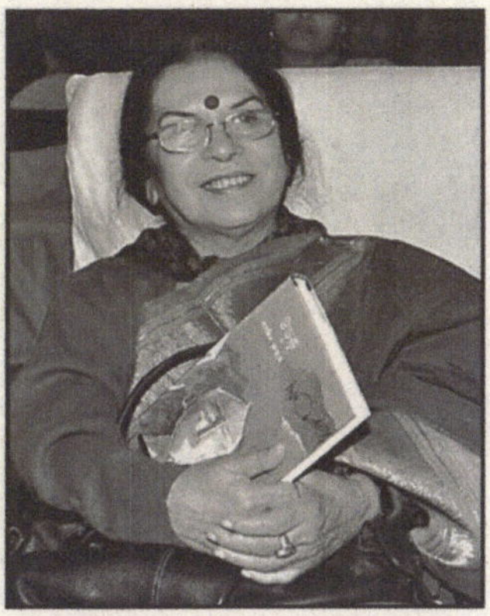

Bani Basu is arguably the most versatile contemporary writer in Bengali, the broad range of her fiction deals with gender, history, mythology, society, psychology, adolescence, music, sexual orientation, the supernatural, and more. Besides writing novels and short stories, she is also an essayist, critic and poet. She has won a number of literary awards, including the Sahitya Akademi award. She lives and writes in Calcutta.

A NOTE ON THE TRANSLATOR

Arunava Sinha translates classic, modern and contemporary Bengali fiction and non-fiction into English. Twenty-eight of his translated works have been published so far. Born and brought up in Calcutta, he lives and works in Delhi.